THE SAN LUIS RANGE

THE SAN LUIS RANGE

Lauran Paine

GUNSMOKE

First published in the UK by Foulsham

This hardback edition 2009
by BBC Audiobooks Ltd
by arrangement with
Golden West Literary Agency

ISBN 978 1 408 46238 6

British Library Cataloguing in Publication Data available.

Printed and bound in Great Britain by
CPI Antony Rowe, Chippenham and Eastbourne

Chapter One

Jefferson Mordant was a strongly built, tallish man with a ruddy face. At thirty there were no tell-tale lines indicating the inherent drives within him; the gnawing compulsions. He was a plain-looking man; taciturn, thin-lipped, supple and hard-eyed. Now, he stood back with impatience waiting for Al Waters to notice him.

The store was busy; customers stood about, talked, handled merchandise, acted impatient and Al Waters saw Mordant in the background, threw him a brusque nod and rolled his head sideways towards a door marked Office.

Mordant wove through the customers, pushed past the door and dropped into a cane-bottomed chair. It was stifling hot in the office with both windows closed. When Waters came in a moment later he gave the door an annoyed shove behind him, fixed blue eyes on Mordant and waited. Early morning was a bad time for interruptions. People did their shopping before the heat became unbearable.

When Mordant didn't speak Waters said: "I got your note, Jeff."

The cowman's voice was clipped, authoritative. "It's about the Pacheco grant, Al." Mordant eyed the merchant dispassionately.

"What about it?"

"You own five thousand acres adjoining Pacheco on the west. I've got that leased. I own fifteen thousand acres adjoining both your land and Pacheco."

"And?"

"It isn't enough land, Al."

"No? Well; you've got all the San Luis foothills and the malpais back yonder as out-range, haven't you?"

"That's not the point. Three days ago I rode to Salt Lick for strays. There were two wagons there. Homesteaders setting up shacks right—goddammit—in the middle of my winter graze."

Waters settled on the edge of a table, swung one leg irritably. "You can handle them. You've handled them before."

Mordant shook his head slowly. "Burning out emigrants is like a range fire. The grass comes back. I used to think it was a good way. I don't think so any more."

Waters's eyes blanked over, grew introspective. "Every day more wagons, more people. It's plain enough, Jeff. The San Luis country is changing. Pretty soon——"

"Pretty soon cowmen'll have to fight the whole United States to keep their range rights."

"Right—so?"

"I went down to Raton and studied the tax files. Squatters have filed for homesteads on your five thousand acres and in pieces I've neglected getting titles to on my fifteen thousand acres."

Waters's gaze grew still, sharp. "How could they? I got title."

"You've got blind spots—pieces—quarter sections, a dab here, a dab there, that've never been proved up on. You figured like I did. By owning surrounding sections the inside land was safe from trespass. Well; it isn't. There's laws of egress. Those clodhoppers can cross your grass, and mine, to get to those blind spots, and homestead them. The law says so."

Waters was silent a long time. Mordant built a cigarette, lit it and exhaled. Smoke hung in the heavy atmosphere.

"Al, I've called for a re-appraisal of the Pacheco grant.

I'm claiming the grant's eighty thousand acres is more'n the Pacheco family needs to run what stock they have—or ever will have. It's perfectly legal. It's written right in the law that when the United States confirmed titles to those old Spanish grants, they were subject to re-appraisal."

"I see," Waters said. "It boils down to getting a slice of Pacheco to off-set what the grangers have homesteaded."

"That's right." Jeff eased his six-gun away from the chair's side where it gouged him. "And this is where you come in. The government will send a man out here to make an investigation. You own adjoining land. So does Matt Reynolds. He adjoins Pacheco on the south. You and Matt and me stand to benefit from the breaking up of the Pacheco grant. Now then—are you interested in buying more land?"

Waters frowned slightly. "I guess so. The country's growing. But how much will it go for by the acre? At best it's a long-term investment."

Mordant swiped sweat off his chin with a shirtsleeve. "That depends," he said. "While I was down at Raton I nosed around a little. They tell me these investigators can be bought. That's why I went to see Matt last night and came around to see you this morning. It's 'way too much for one man to handle. We'll make up a pot to bribe this feller, get him to condemn the grant and keep his mouth shut until the day of the sale. The three of us'll be in Raton that day, buy up what land we want and let the devil have the rest."

Waters laced his fingers together and let them lie in his lap. His eyes were unblinkingly remote looking. After a while he sighed and quirked a humourless smile at Mordant.

"How much do you want—and when do you want it?"

The cowman heaved himself up out of the chair. "Nothing yet," he said, starting towards the door.

On an impulse Waters turned. "Wait a minute. Let's go talk to Matt."

The cowman gazed downward. An ironic expression appeared in his eyes. "Come on," he said.

Waters held the door open and said, "Damned abstract office can't be any busier'n my place."

They passed between stacked counters, beyond the harassed glances of two clerks and out on to the scuffed duckboards, heavy with human traffic. Under a lemon-yellow sun the village of San Luis had an undercurrent of hurry despite the sunblasting heat.

Mordant swung into the lead, skirted through the roadway's traffic of jogging horsemen, democrat wagons, buggies, firing sentences at Waters, whose shorter legs made hard work of the dusty crossing.

"Those Pachecos are like all pepper-bellies. Sit around in the sun. Run a few scrawny Mex cattle. Let the world go past them. Hell; five thousand acres is all they'll ever need."

Waters grunted when he stepped up on to the duckboards across the roadway; said nothing.

"Never amounted to a damn," Mordant went on, "and never will. They won't grow with the country—people like that—and the country's growing. People have got to look ahead; plan their futures. Especially cowmen; if they don't there won't be enough open country left to run stock on."

A lean, bronzed man swung past, nodded, a nickel badge on his shirt inscribed Deputy Marshal. Mordant returned the nod. "Howdy, Burt."

Waters's gaze lingered on the deputy marshal. When he was up beside Mordant he said, "It's got to be kept legal, Jeff."

Mordant rested a hand on the latch of a door lettered San Luis Land and Abstract Company. "I told you it was legal," he said shortly.

8

"Sure, I know. That's something you don't want to lose sight of. The San Luis country is growing in lots of ways. Gun law isn't any good any more. There's a book law now." He looked up into the ruddy face, saw the hardness of the grey eyes and shook his head a little. "I don't mean Marshal Grant or Deputy Marshal Joyce. I mean Federal law down at Raton. Troops and lawyers—honest to God Territorial law. U.S. law, Jeff. It isn't *all* for sale."

Mordant didn't reply. He shoved his way inside, shot a glance at the clerks and customers and headed for the cubbyhole office beyond.

Matthew Reynolds was an incredibly thin, tall man. His movements were rickety, the eyes diluted blue and hung far back under a baulk of forehead with scraggly hair above it. He blinked at Jeff, jerked his head a little, studied Al Waters's face and leaned back in his chair.

"What's up, boys?"

Mordant sank into a chair and bobbed his head at Waters, who sat down, cleared his throat and looked uncomfortable. "Jeff's been talking to me about the Pacheco grant, Matt."

"Oh," Reynolds said non-committally, waiting.

Mordant said: "I explained it all to him."

Reynolds put skeletal hands behind his head. "What do you think, Al? How's it sound to you?"

"Well; from what Jeff says it sounds like a good enough opportunity." Waters squinted, a single droplet of perspiration forming on his chin. "Have you ever been through one of these land re-appraisals, Matt; what're they like?"

Reynolds looked amused. "You mean how much will the bribe be, don't you?" He didn't wait for an answer. "It's hard to say. Maybe a thousand dollars. Maybe five thousand. Depends on the amount of land involved and the appraiser. We won't know until we talk to this bird. I've been in on several re-appraisals though, when those government men *have* been bribed." Reynolds took a thin Mexican cigar from a drawer, lit it and blew smoke into the humid atmosphere.

"I'm sure it can be worked, but with me that's secondary. The important question is just how much is that land worth." The pale eyes left Waters, flicked to Mordant's face. "What do you think, Jeff?"

With no hesitation Mordant said, "I'll give a dollar an acre for as much of Pacheco as I can get."

Waters frowned. "Wait a minute. Let's understand one thing right now. Just how are we going to divide this land."

Reynolds looked down at his hands. "Jeff; did you say you'd specified an amount in your complaint?"

"No. It wasn't a complaint anyway, just a request for a re-appraisal."

Matt looked up. "Good. The Pacheco family controls eighty thousand acres. I'd say twenty thousand is ample for their needs. What would you say, Jeff?"

"More than enough."

"That leaves sixty thousand acres to be declared excess by the Federal man. How about twenty thousand apiece?"

Jeff and Waters nodded in thoughtful silence.

Reynolds was gazing at his hands again when he said, "Jeff; what's Pacheco's brand, I've forgotten."

"They call it Tres Cruz. Three Cross or Three Crosses. One small cross, a bigger cross and another small cross. What about it?"

Reynolds's face showed interest. "The Trinity," he said.

Waters was making a cigarette. He looked up. "The what?"

"Trinity. It's a religious symbol."

Mordant was losing interest, gazing at a calendar on the wall when he said. "Old Epifanio Pacheco once told me it was the brand of Cortez."

Reynolds nodded softly. "The brand of Cortez . . ." His hobby was the history of the land. Veering back to the matter on hand he dropped a clanger. "Gentlemen; I've been thinking about this deal since last night and I'm not prepared to put such a sum of money into this land, so if either of you want a slice of my one-third you're welcome to it."

Mordant and Waters looked shocked. The cowman finally spoke. "The San Luis is growing, Matt. Five years from now that land'll be worth two, maybe three dollars an acre."

Reynolds said, "Sure; I agree, Jeff, but I just can't tie up so much money and wait five years to get it back." He stroked the back of his head. "You and Al are fixed differently. Look at it this way; you'll lease Al's land and that will make him money. Then you'll increase your herd, which will make *you* money. Me—I'm saddled with twenty thousand acres of land that won't net me a red cent for five years at the very least."

Jeff Mordant was frowning. "I'll lease your one-third from you, Matt, just like I'll do with Al." The grey eyes were like flint. "Get title to that land and I'll give you a five year lease, pay two years in advance and take an option to buy."

Reynolds studied the ruddy face for a moment, then inclined his head. "That's different. You didn't make that offer last night. All right; on that basis I'll stay in for a third."

Waters stood up, fidgeted. "You fellows don't need me any more and the store's packed. How soon will we have to make up our kitty to bribe this fellow with?"

Reynolds shrugged, "Not until after one of us has sounded him out. I'll let you know how much, later. All right?"

"Yes. One last thing; this is just between the three of us and no talking about it to anyone else."

"Certainly."

From Mordant a nod.

Satisfied, the merchant left. Jeff watched him go and it would have been impossible for him to define his feelings towards Al Waters right then. He faced the abstractor. "That makes it easier on all of us, three pardners instead of two."

Reynolds smiled. "Just as well. I couldn't lay my hands on that kind of money without borrowing and for a deal like this borrowing is out."

Mordant stood up, unsmiling and predatory looking. "You'll make enough off this deal to go fishing for a couple of years," he said, and walked out closing the door behind him.

He teetered on the edge of the duckboards and watched the sweating turmoil of San Luis a long moment. The sun was almost overhead. The only shade was under the overhangs that fronted most of the stores. He crossed through the powdery dust to the shadows under the Emerald Slipper Saloon's overhang, stared a moment at the A. L. Waters mercantile building, then shouldered past the louvred doors. They shuddered on oiled spindles at his passage.

It was musty-cool inside. Men hung limply over the bar making desultory, subdued conversation. A few were at tables nursing glasses of beer. The day bartender, called Rusty because of the colour of his hair and freckles, moved towards Mordant with a blank, disinterested expression. Jeff ordered ale. It came, tepid and slightly sour. He drank without seeing himself in the back bar mirror. An idea was nagging him; impatience gnawed at the delay. He'd waited ten years to have enough money to acquire part of Pacheco's grant. Now the time was close and he stormed inwardly at the wait ahead. He tilted the glass back, drained it and struck the bar with it, sharply. Rusty hustled a re-fill. Jeff drank that one slower, plumbing ways to expedite what lay ahead. When the ale was gone he flipped a coin on the bar and walked back outside and down towards Waters's store. There was a way to make things more certain, at that.

Al was in his office when Jeff entered. He looked up. Jeff dumped himself into a chair, made a cigarette, lit it and exhaled. "After we broke up I got an idea. Pacheco's got about five hundred head. I think that might look like too many critters to this government man. I've got a couple of riders I can trust who'll run off a couple hundred head."

Waters looked startled. "That's rustling, Jeff."

"No. I'll just have them driven back into the hills until they're footsore. They'll eventually drift back, but not until the re-appraisal's over with."

"But Pacheco'll tell the land man how many head he has."

Jeff bent a withering glance at Waters. "Sure he will, and the land man'll expect him to lie about the amount of stock he has. I'll say Pacheco has a couple of hundred head. You and Matt'll say the same thing. Where'll that leave Pacheco?"

Waters gazed at the wall. Being associated with Jeff Mordant was nothing he would have personally sought. There were a lot of stories; Jeff was a fast man with a gun, a vindictive enemy, a bad man to cross. Waters wondered if he might not be a bad man to be in collusion with.

"What's Matt say?"

"He'll go along."

Waters fidgeted. "I'm no cowman, but won't there be ways to find out?"

"Sure. After the appraiser's gone the cattle will start drifting back. By then Pacheco'll suspect. What do we care what he thinks? What a man can't prove he'd better not say."

The risk was Mordant's, of course. Waters's eyes dropped to the smooth, dark face. "When'll the land agent show up?"

A shrug. "Who knows? A few days; a week maybe. I'll get rid of the cattle and if he doesn't show up for a week they'll still be a long way from home."

"Is it really necessary, Jeff? There's likely to be danger——"

"No danger," Mordant interrupted, rising. "They'll be driven across JM range where I've got every right to drive *any* cattle and no one'll know what happened until afterwards."

Mordant left and Al Waters sat perfectly motionless, earlier elation souring.

Mordant left San Luis riding north and west over the rolling-to-flat country. The sun bore down, perspiration ran under his clothing. The distance swam and eventually, when he was on his own range, the cattle he saw, branded JM, right rib, in block letters seared into the living flesh, were panting, lifeless looking, hugging shade where they could find it.

The heat didn't bother Mordant much. His eyes were squinted under the tugged-forward brim of his hat, not so much from glare as from thought. A vision of empire quickened in his mind.

He rode over the tinder dry range to a slight knoll and reined up under an unkempt old oak. Southward lay the immense solitude of the Pacheco grant. His lips grew thin, his eyes unmoving, hot looking.

Below, next to a creek and beneath some clustered cottonwoods, three riders lounged near a semi-permanent, unhitched wagon. The equipment indigenous to all cow-camps lay scattered. A little way off horses grazed, hobbled.

There was a difference between a cowman and a rancher. Jeff Mordant was a cowman. His camp was wherever JM cattle drifted on an unfenced expanse of range. He kept a room at the Emerald Slipper Hotel in San Luis but his home was the JM cow-camp, his desk and office the saddle, his walls the eternity of grassland.

With a careless flick of the reins he started down towards the camp. A rider saw him coming, said something to his companions. One was playing solitaire on a stiff saddle blanket. Another was sprawled asleep in the shade. He rolled over, sat up and spat, watched Jeff dismount, unsaddle, dip a drink from the water bucket, spit, and walk towards the wagon.

In the shade Jeff dropped down limply, tossed his hat aside and swiped at his forehead. A mass of handsome, chestnut hair was pressed against his head. He gazed hoodedly at the three riders. The man playing solitaire was squat, slope shouldered; a 'breed out of Texas. He had muddy eyes and a laughingly cruel mouth. Of them all only the 'breed wore two guns. Jeff knew Garra well.

"'Tonio; catch me a fresh horse and saddle him, will you?"

The two-gun man pushed erect, grunted and started away. He wore ornate Chihuahua spurs that rang with a warm sound.

Jeff turned to the remaining two men. Both were lean, hard faced, sinewy men. One, called Caleb, had a badly pock-marked face and a slit of a mouth, perpetually chapped. He was also a Texan, and of the three riders Caleb understood Jeff Mordant the best. He sat there, now, waiting, knowing something was in the wind.

The third man was quite a few years younger than either Antonio Garra or Caleb. Although his face was as yet unlined it was burnt a dark mahogany colour. His eyes were quick-moving and dark brown. Like Mordant and Caleb, the younger rider, called Enos, wore only one gun, but in keeping with Southwestern practice Enos, like the others, carried a knife in a small holster stitched into the outside upper of his boot.

Jeff considered the younger man. The other two were perfectly reliable, bothered by neither scruples or ethics, devoid of consciences. He cleared his throat and began to speak, never letting his gaze leave Enos's face. He wanted two hundred or so of Pacheco's cattle rounded up and driven far back into the malpais country; over the roughest, rockiest ground. When he was finished he waited, still watching the young rider. The first to speak was Caleb.

"Should've been done years ago," Caleb said. "Keep those Mex bulls away from JM cows."

Jeff said, "What d'you think, Enos?"

"Reckon so," the youth replied slowly. "Pacheco's too big for an old man an' a skinny kid to run." He paused, then said: "But, suppose someone sees us moving those Three Cross critters . . ." He let it hang there unfinished, watching Jeff.

Caleb snorted. "We got a right," he said. "Three Crosses're always drifting over on to our range."

Jeff tossed his head to elude a drowsy but interested fly, picked up his hat and held it. "We're not rustling Three Cross cattle, Enos," he said. "Just pushing them out of our way. Nothing illegal." He didn't believe this was bothering the youth as much as being *seen* driving a neighbour's cattle into rough country was. "Anyway, since we've been so hard on trespassers lately—since those homesteaders have come in—I don't imagine we'll have an audience."

Enos looked convinced. "When do we drive them?"

"The sooner the better," Jeff said getting to his feet. "We'll spend the afternoon gathering them. Start the drive by moonlight; be in the malpais by dawn and from there only eagles will see us." He stood there gazing at Enos. Caleb arose, dusted his britches and waited for the younger

16

man. Antonio Garra was coming towards them leading a fresh horse with Mordant's rigging on it. Jeff swung slowly and looked at Caleb.

"Let's get mounted up. While you two are saddling I'll talk to 'Tonio."

He watched them walk past the 'breed, stretched his arm for the reins and said, "'Tonio; we're going to round up couple hundred head of Pacheco's cattle and drive them back into the malpais. Get 'em footsore enough so they'll be a week getting back." He pulled the reins slowly through his fingers looking after the other two riders. "Tell me something; what we're going to do isn't illegal—but will Enos keep his mouth shut, later?"

"Sure," the 'breed said with gusty emphasis. "He's all right. Ain't been many places but he ain't very old either. He's all right, Jeff."

Temporarily shelving the matter Mordant dropped his gaze to the 'breed's face. "What about you?" he said.

Garra looked surprised then he shrugged. "Me? Anything's better'n sitting around here playing cards and sewing saddles." Garra smiled with startling effect. White teeth, large and even, made a brilliant flash in the swarthiness of his face. He passed a salt-stiff sleeve over his forehead. "I know where there's better'n two hundred Three Crosses. Seen 'em yesterday. Over by Salt Lick."

Jeff jerked the horse in closer, spoke as he toed into the stirrup. "That'll save gathering. Get your horse, 'Tonio."

They rode north-east through the sweltering humidity until dark blotches against the tan earth stood out. Little bunches of cattle standing in the shade of one another. When the four riders topped out over a lift their scent travelled almost as rapidly as the sight of them did. The Tres Cruz cattle, seldom handled and retaining much of the wildness of Spanish cattle, fled. Antonio Garra, easily the best cowboy of the four riders, laughed and loped away to turn the animals into the west, towards the lowering sun with purplish hills below it, dancing and twisting in the fierce heat.

There was no wasted motion. Caleb made a big sashay so as to come in on the wing of the turning cattle. Jeff and Enos fell wide, leaving the trail westward open. When Garra spun in at the leaders the animals alternated between a confused, shambling trot, and bursts of speed. The heat was too de-energising and an hour later with a minimum of dust the Tres Cruz critters were strung out, swinging due west towards the malpais country far off.

Jeff saw Enos swipe at his glistening face with a sleeve, not once but every few minutes. The grey eyes slitted thoughtfully again. Jeff let the youth alone; the drive kept him occupied. He counted close to three hundred head. To rectify this he deliberately let an occasional critter double back, deducting each cut-back as he rode until there were no more than two hundred Tres Cruz animals ahead of him.

A choking pall of cow-dust hung horse high over the herd and fell back, thick enough to chew, strong enough to smell. Jeff and Caleb cursed it. Garra, far ahead at the point, rode like a man enjoying himself. There was no dust at the point. Enos rode with a mouth sprung and gash-like in his bronzed face.

When the sun dropped bloody-red behind the farthest escarpment they were still travelling due west, still with Antonio Garra up ahead, one thick, short leg dangling free of stirrup, big hat dumped far back, an occasional careless wave thrown back to the gritty-eyed men in the drag and on the wings.

The Tres Cruz cattle, wicked-horned, slab-sided, almost every colour and combination of colours, clicked horns as they shuffled through their own dust. Coats dark with sweat, eyes red, tongues lolling, at the first fringe of cha-

18

parral they lowered their heads and crashed through to rid themselves of the myriad horn-and-heel-flies. Near the heavy brush the air was cooler.

Later, Garra dropped from sight far ahead, following some ancient game trail. The Spanish cattle had long since accepted his leadership, were strung out in his wake.

Enos threw a long, relieved glance over the range when the brush came up, closing down around men and beasts. He hung limp in the saddle. He sucked a great, fetid lungful of breath into his lungs, felt his eyes squeak with grit as he swung them in a long scrutiny of the countryside, and off to his left sitting a horse atop a broken lip of landswell, was a solitary horseman. Enos's heart crashed painfully, once, in its cage. His breath caught, hung in his throat and he looked frantically around for Jeff. Mordant and Caleb were riding stirrup to stirrup, saying nothing, heads down, handkerchiefs over their lower faces.

All the fear Enos had felt since Salt Lick, returned, crept into his throat and constricted it. He wanted to yell at Jeff. Instead he swung back and pinpointed the watching stranger.

The horseman reined out along the broken swell and looked down at the animals nearest him, then he straightened up and watched the oncoming riders. Enos's nerves were like skinned snakes. He threw another frightened glance at Jeff, but Mordant was angling north-west out of the dust and Caleb was riding beside him. Enos swung down, clawed out his carbine, knelt and shouldered it. Sweat stung his eyes.

The tawny sunlight on the carbine barrel must have heliographed a warning to the stranger. As the sights moved to bear the horseman whirled, jumped his horse out and disappeared down the far side of the swell. Enos fired, holding low, just before the man went out of sight. The flat explosion was doubly sharp and loud in the brittle air.

Cattle bawled and after a moment there was the drum-roll rumble of their running.

Caleb jerked erect at the shot. Jeff Mordant swung his dust-streaked mount and spurred towards Enos, face dun coloured above the rag over nose and mouth, grey eyes dry looking, unblinking.

"What did you shoot at?"

Enos stood up. Sweat was running copiously under his shirt and he hugged the carbine barrel at his side. "A feller was sitting up there on that broken ridge watching us." Avoiding Mordant's stare Enos turned, shoved the gun back into its boot. "A Tres Cruz man sure as hell."

Jeff could almost smell the fear and it angered him. He'd get rid of Enos; had to. Regardless of what Garra thought Enos didn't have sand enough in his craw for a JM rider. Pay him off and get him a long way from the San Luis country. He watched Enos mount, finger his reins and finally point at a clump of manzanita.

"Over there. East of that brush patch. That's where he went out of sight."

Jeff heard Caleb rein up behind him. He looked around, jerked his head and said, "Come on."

The three of them were going up the gradual slope of the swell when Antonio Garra came, sweat darkened and spurring, through the chaparral. His face was an adobe coloured questionmark. Enos was riding behind Caleb. Garra edged past him, swung in beside Caleb and asked who had fired and why?

Jeff rode ahead as far as the manzanita clump. There he reined up, closed both hands over the horn and sat like stone looking downward. When the 'breed and Caleb drew close, Enos trailing them, Antonio let off a blast of startled profanity. All four of them sat looking down at a big black horse, breedy looking and very dead.

Jeff exhaled slowly.

"Right through the heart."

Caleb was motionless until the last word died, then, with a fluid movement he slid off his horse, stood close and peered at the surrounding brush across the saddle-seat. "Where's the rider?" he asked shortly.

Jeff's angry gaze swept the brush. He made no movement to dismount or unclasp his hands. After a moment he said, "You and Enos track him down. Can't be far. Take him back to the cow camp and keep him out of sight. 'Tonio and I'll finish the drive." He fixed Enos with a long stare then swung abruptly towards the distant mountains. Garra trailed after him.

Much later, just before the last light failed altogether, Jeff topped a thin shift of brushy hogback and gazed back the way he had come. His steadily burning wrath found a shred of satisfaction in picturing Enos beating the brush for the man whose horse he'd shot, scairt stiff and shaking.

Jeff made a cigarette. The range was hazily cool now and nothing moved as far as he could see. Except for the idiocy of Enos the drive was thus far successful. He twisted, searching for the shape of Garra, didn't find him and rode leisurely after the last of the leg-weary Tres Cruz cattle.

When the moon came up Jeff watched it. It was thick in the middle, sharp ends slanting upwards into the sky. A Comanche moon; the light wasn't white but it was sufficient in a soft, glowing way. Twice he heard Garra sing out and yodelled back.

The cattle had no fight or stampede left in them. They were tired, foot-sore and thirsty. Old cows hung back. Jeff used his romal to sting them along and by dawn his left arm ached from swinging the thing.

Antonio Garra materialised out of the brush, swarthy face a mask of layered dust and sweat, mud-coloured eyes bloodshot looking. He pointed a thick arm where the cattle were trampling a thin stream, milling eagerly, snatching mouthfuls of tough ripgut grass and slavering over it.

"'Sta bueno, Jefe."

Jeff reined up, dropped the reins over the horn and groped for his tobacco sack. "Sons of bitches," he said hoarsely.

Antonio looked around at him quickly, not knowing what Jeff meant. He said nothing. Raised his shoulders and let them fall.

"How long'll it take them to get back, 'Tonio?"

Another shrug, understanding this time. "Three, four days maybe. They're wore out. They'll rest today and tomorrow. Maybe start back day after tomorrow."

"That's too soon."

Garra watched the cattle, avoided looking at Jeff. "There is a barranca ahead a little ways. We could push them down it. As hot as it is now they won't even try to climb back up here for a long time."

"Let's go," Jeff said. "When you get to the top wait there for me. No sense in pointing them all the way down, we'll drive them down together."

Garra swung back through the prickly brush and Jeff's horse plodded heavily under the guidance of its rider. The cattle were hard to drive away from the creek; harder to keep from breaking back. By the time Jeff got to the barranca he was dull with fatigue. It irked him the way Garra and his horse seemed so fresh in spite of their dried sweat. He made a cigarette up on the plateau and used up the last of his horse turning bolters, edging the critters over the lip of the barranca and down a buck-run into the grass-land far below. By the time the last animal was going down Garra made a wide grin, drew up and dropped his reins, slack.

"A week, maybe as much as two weeks before they get back up out of there."

Jeff turned his horse without wasting a moment looking down into the shadowy lowlands, arroyos, cienages, where Pacheco's cattle were fanning out. "Come on," he said. "I'm hungrier'n a bear cub."

Garra followed, using weight and knees to steer his horse while he curled up a lumpy cigarette, popped it into his mouth and lit it. He looked comfortable and satisfied, incredibly dirty and Indian-like, untired.

It took them until nearly midnight to make it back to the cow camp. Their horses were totally exhausted. Enos and Caleb were lying in their soogans smoking when they rode up, swung down, turned their horses loose and rummaged through the pans at the fire for remnants to make a meal of. Garra stoked up the fire under the coffeepot and out of the night Enos's thin voice said, "We never found him, Jeff."

Jeff ignored the words, went to his saddle, tugged out the wet saddleblanket, spread it out on the ground and lay back without speaking. His jaws worked ponderously over tough, cold venison, grey eyes unseeingly on the overhead, hard and steady. Garra poured a tin cup full of coffee and put it beside Jeff. Some time later, when the edge was off his hunger, Jeff drank the coffee, rinsed his mouth and spat. Then he spoke.

"Why'd you shoot at him, Enos?"

The answer came right back, pat. "He looked like Ramon Pacheco. Same skinny build and that black horse . . ."

Jeff cursed in tight, explosive profanity. "If it *was* young Pacheco—what of it? We weren't breaking any law clearing JM range of Tres Cruz cattle—you damned fool. If you've shot him there'll be hell to pay—and for no reason at all."

"I didn't hit him," Enos said thinly. "Caleb and I tracked him close to the Pacheco place. There wasn't any blood and no staggering. He wasn't hurt; just the horse got killed. We went back to look at the brand, had to roll it over."

"And?"

Caleb said: "There wasn't no brand, Jeff."

Jeff turned his head, looked into the older rider's face. Neither of them spoke for a while then Jeff said, "No brand?"

"Nope." Caleb scratched his head. "I got an idea. That wasn't young Pacheco, it was a stranger."

Jeff's nostrils quivered. "Oh, Lord," he said, then he swore viciously at Enos. "If it was Ramon Pacheco he and the old man would have gone to San Luis and raised hell with the marshal. If it was a stranger, he'll tell the Pachecos what he saw—direction we were driving the Tres Cruzes. All our work'll be wasted." He started to curse again. Antonio Garra came back from sluicing off at the creek. He stood beside Jeff dripping water.

"We could ride over an' see if Ramon got hurt."

Jeff slanted a glance up at him. "You heard Enos say he had a good look at us, didn't you? Well; the first JM man who rides into Pacheco's yard'll get shot at."

Garra wagged his head, grinning. "Not me," he said. "I was out of sight up ahead in the chaparral. He didn't see me, Jeff."

Mordant's gaze closed down on Antonio's face and he nodded gently. "That's sound, 'Tonio," he said. "You're dead right. All right; first thing in the morning you ride over; say you're looking for a stray horse. See if there's a stranger around or if Ramon's hurt."

Garra's chin dripped creek water. For a long time he stood looking down at Jeff, the smile intact, glistening, then he

24

turned towards his own bedroll. "All right. You going to wait until I get back?"

"Yeah. 'Won't go to town tomorrow anyway. Too dog-gut tired for one thing. Got some firing to do, for another thing."

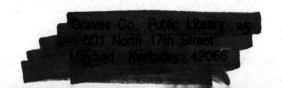

Chapter Two

The home of Epifanio Pacheco was as ageless as the land itself. It was low, thick-walled adobe. There were signs of weathering where the wide overhang of roof eaves didn't quite keep spring rains from eroding earthen walls. Stone walkways around the main home were smooth from generations of boots and moccasins. Great cottonwoods and oaks made purple shadows around the buildings. Permanence soaked into riders approaching the ranch. Permanence of land and sky and a certain timelessness that was inherently Southwestern-Spanish.

There were also, aside from the old house and low, adobe barn, a blacksmith shop, a smoke house, a neglected bunkhouse of adobe used now by the last of the Pacheco vaqueros, an ancient Indian, and a cool, vine-covered spring house.

When Antonio Garra rode into the yard he saw three men and a woman sitting on benches in the heavily shaded main patio. The sun made the range shimmer, daubed glittering shafts of lemon-yellow brilliance over the surrounding country but failed to penetrate where the people were. Antonio slouched in his saddle, muddy eyes moving, probing, studying; a lone horseman, thick-bodied, two-gunned and slit-eyed.

A whipcord thin and stringy vaquero appeared noiselessly in the doorway of the bunkhouse as Garra approached. Black eyes studied the 'breed impassively. Garra nodded amiably enough.

"Buenos dias, viejo," he said. The Indian grunted and

nodded, waiting. Garra's glance flashed to the people on the patio, watching him. He raised his voice a little and spoke to the vaquero. "Lost two JM horses. Thought they might have come this way."

The ancient vaquero wagged his head laconically, watching Garra out of sunken, unblinking eyes. He leaned against the door jamb and said, "No, señor. There have been no stray horses come here in a long, long time. Your horses must have gone elsewhere."

Garra reined up in silence, studying the people on the patio. He made out Epifanio Pacheco's lean, shrivelled form, and his son, Ramon's, lithe gracefulness. The girl, he thought, looked familiar. After a moment it came to him. Lola Valdez, a distant cousin of the Pachecos. The fourth person, though, was unfamiliar to him. He squinted hard. The man had thick legs in tight levis, massively broad shoulders and a head that was sideways, presenting a bony, harsh profile. Antonio's attention was drawn back to the vaquero who was watching him.

"Would you care to speak to Don Epifanio?" The black old eyes were snake-like in their stillness, and shrewd appearing. Garra looked down at the old man, knew he was being chided for staring, grunted and dismounted. Without answering he left his horse and went towards the people on the patio. Epifanio Pacheco rose, met Garra at the edge of the stone walk. He was very old, like the vaquero, with eyes just as black. His face was drawn tight, lips thinned with pressure. There was hostility in the old Spaniard's look and Garra stopped before it, hooked thumbs in his shell-belt and asked again about stray horses. They stood five feet apart watching one another. Pacheco answered finally, his voice dry, like a hot summer breeze rustling dead grass.

"Stray horses? No, we haven't seen them. What colour were they, Garra?"

27

Antonio never faltered. "Sorrels. Two sorrels, Señor."

Pacheco's eyes widened a trifle. "Not black, Garra?"

Uneasiness stirred in the 'breed. "No; they were sorrels," he said doggedly.

"We haven't seen them."

Garra shifted his weight, thinking, then he turned with a stingy nod, went to his horse, mounted and wheeled out of the yard.

The Indian watched Garra ride out into the smashing sunlight, then started towards the patio. Epifanio Pacheco stood like a reed, watching Garra's dust. When the Indian was close he removed his battered sombrero but in his face was the easy and confident familiarity of lifelong servitude. Before he could speak Ramon Pacheco crossed the patio to his father's side. He was dark eyed and haired but with creamy white skin. He raised eyebrows at the vaquero.

"As you figured," the Indian said in soft Spanish. "He looks for two horses that he assuredly never lost and he looks up here all the time he is riding in."

Epifanio Pacheco's seamed face, burnt prune colour from lifelong sunblasting, held dark eyes slitted in calculation. He turned a little and gazed at the powerful man still sitting with Lola Valdez back in the shade. "There is your answer, amigo. Garra is one of Mordant's three riders."

The big man stood up and nodded. "His visit's almost as good as an admission, isn't it?"

Old Epifanio's eyes swept to the girl and back to the stranger. "Again—why? It is awfully hot to be driving other people's cattle. What is the purpose?" He turned away from the Indian, crossed the patio to a bench and sank down. "We have discussed it at great length and always we come back to—why? Not to get Tres Cruz animals off JM range. For that they would be driven south—over here—not west so that when they drift back they'll still be on JM range. And never before so far nor so secretly. What's behind it, then?" He looked around. No one spoke until Ramon made a gesture with one hand.

"The main thing is to get our cattle back."

Epifanio bobbed his head curtly. "Of course. You are right." He looked out where the vaquero stood. "Three horses, Juan. Ramon, Señor Donnellen, and I will ride this afternoon, when it cools."

The old Indian didn't move. His coal black eyes hung unwaveringly upon the old Spaniard's face. There was a moment of awkward silence then Pacheco shrugged. "All right, Juan. Four horses then." The Indian nodded and walked away. Cliff Donnellen watched the old vaquero walking back across the yard; he laughed. Epifanio shrugged and spread his hands. There was humour in the wry face he made. "It is always the same," he said. "He gets what he wants without ever asking."

Lola Valdez looked amused too. Her beauty was singularly like that of an old painting. Rich in colouring, soft-shadowed; a kind of beauty to make the blood run faster; the kind of beauty that Spain alone bequeaths. Moreover, there was an indefinable toughness to Lola Valdez. Something that was felt; a sort of Southwestern aura of rawhide, of toughness and hardihood that came up out of the land itself.

Cliff Donnellen leaned forward on his bench. "If you'd loan me a horse," he said to Epifanio, "I'd like to ride into San Luis before we go after your cattle."

Ramon stood up. "Of course," he said, then, aside to his father: "No need for you to bother, I'll catch one."

Lola Valdez spoke for the first time, looking up at Donnellen. "You'll be back early enough for supper?"

He looked straight into her eyes when he answered. "If I have to fly," he said, and flashed her a wide smile.

Epifanio watched Donnellen and his son walk across the

yard towards the corrals. He sighed and said, "The old and the new, Lola."

Her dark glance was puzzled. "The old and the new?"

A gesture with one blue-veined hand towards his son and the bigger man beside him. "Yes. Ramon—not so large but graceful. Hard and sparse from the old land. Señor Donnellen—big and powerful and very confident in his walk. In the way he looks at you. In the way he carries his head —in himself. He is the new blood in our land, Ramon is the old blood."

The girl's glance swept past the old man and studied the walking figures. Donnellen was larger, of course, and his chest was wide beneath the massive shoulders, but he walked flat on his feet while Ramon walked lightly. "At least," she said, "his blood might be better blood than Mordant's."

Epifanio laughed. It sounded like shale in a waterfall. Musical—but brittle, hollow, and a little sad. "Possibly, Lola," he said and regarded the girl obliquely for a second. "He likes you, niña."

Her head came around quickly. In Spanish she said: "Are you thinking the old blood should be crossed with the new, then?"

This time his laughter was appreciative and warm. "The new blood may be thicker, little one, but the wit is not so quick, is it?"

They sat there watching the rider trotting across the yard. When Donnellen threw them a wave they both responded and Epifanio nodded unconsciously. "He rides well," he said.

The girl's eyes followed the rider until he was lost in the dancing heatwaves then she got up abruptly and started towards the door.

Alone, Epifanio slouched in the shade looking into the distance without seeing. There had to be a reason for Mor-

30

dant to drive off his cattle like that, but what was it? He'd pushed drifting Tres Cruz cattle off JM range before, but not westward nor so far. There was more to it, some way. He sighed, pushed himself off the bench, scooped up his hat and ambled towards the barn. For riding in the darkness to the malpais country he wanted the best horses.

His face puckered as he crossed the yard. It was an odd affair, this running off of Tres Cruz cattle. Donnellen had told him enough, his descriptions had been very good. There was no doubt in Epifanio's mind who had driven his animals; Jeff Mordant. He knew about where he would find the cattle, too, so no great damage had been done, but it bothered him, not knowing *why* it had been done. The San Luis had ample grass for everyone. He shook his head and wondered.

And Cliff Donnellen wondered too, as he crossed the Pacheco grant and came down from the northwestern slopes into San Luis. Losing the black horse angered him. Being a stranger in the country made him wary, too, so, before he went after payment for the horse, he wanted to look and listen a little. By prudent effort he managed to share a bench in front of the harness shop with Deputy Marshal Burt Joyce. In the course of their casual conversation in the shade Cliff got a fairly comprehensive picture of the San Luis country, its people and customs. After considerable thought Donnellen said:

"I don't know this country at all. First time I was ever around here. Well—I was riding in from the west about five, six o'clock yesterday evening, and three men driving some Tres Cruz cattle shot my horse out from under me. That is, one of them did the shooting."

The deputy marshal looked around, startled. He studied Donnellen's face a moment then asked: "Where did this happen?"

"About six, eight miles from the Pachecos' place."

31

"You know the Pachecos?"

"Well; I didn't know them until I walked into their yard after I was put afoot. I'm staying over there now—for a day or two, anyway."

"I see," the deputy said. "You wouldn't have any idea who did the shooting, would you?"

Donnellen began to make a cigarette. "Epifanio Pacheco says the description fits Mordant's riders."

Burt Joyce blinked. "Describe 'em," he said.

Cliff described Jeff, Caleb, and Enos, exactly as he'd described them to the Pachecos. Burt Joyce was silent and Donnellen watched him a moment before he said; "I'll get another horse all right. The point is, that black horse was a pretty good friend of mine. I want to know why they shot him."

Joyce said, dryly, "Because they missed *you*, that's plain enough." He got up. "Come on; let's go see the marshal."

Marshal Grant, called "Stumpy" because of his warped legs and brittle way of going, listened in silence then fixed a long, dour look on his deputy. "Burt," he said, "I expect you got an investigation to make, boy. Want to make it this evenin' or before sunup t'morrow."

Burt Joyce looked up, his eyes crinkled in a slow, rueful smile that said you lazy so-and-so as plainly as day. He said, "This evenin'll be fine, Marshal."

Stumpy Grant swung back towards Donnellen. "All right, pardner; we'll look into it for you. If we find out anything or need you, we'll come by Pacheco's."

Donnellen left the office, had two sour mashes at the Emerald Slipper, got into a conversation with a long, lean, rickety man with blue eyes the colour of diluted sky, went with him to the A. L. Waters Mercantile Company and an hour later was hurrying back towards Pacheco's. Lola Valdez over candlelight was something he didn't mean to deprive himself of.

And after he'd left the marshal's office Stumpy Grant rubbed his face and peered over the fingers at Burt Joyce. "Now what's that damned fool up to?" he asked plaintively.

"Mordant?"

"Sure. Hot enough to melt the hubs of hell and *he's* got to stir up something." Grant spat in disgust at a greenish spittoon near his chair, missed as usual, and resumed speaking. "First it was trappers, then it was burning out clodhoppers, then scaring the whey out of legal homesteaders. Now this business of shooting that stranger's horse and running off old Pacheco's scrub cattle."

Burt's crinkle-eyed grin came up. "You're just sore because you might have to ride out there, is all."

"Well—Jeeze: It must be a hundred and fifty degrees in that sun."

"Quit worrying. I'm the guy's going to ride out there anyway, not you."

Irritably the marshal said, "I'm not worrying. After all Jeff's got a right to run off trespassers—I guess."

"Not kill 'em though."

"He didn't. Just shot the feller's horse."

Burt stood up, shoved fisted hands deep into his pockets and said, "That was an accident. Whoever fired that shot didn't aim to miss the man and hit the horse. Not from as far off as Donnellen said they were from him." He looked thoughtfully out the window at the seared roadway. "Well; it'll be cooler out there after sundown."

"Can't see much by moonlight though," Stumpy Grant said dryly.

"Nothing to see anyway. Just a dead horse." The deputy swung back to look at the marshal. "But I'll lay you a bet there's more to it than that, Stumpy. Jeff's a damned smart man. He don't do things without a sound reason—like shooting at this stranger."

Grant picked up some papers off his desk and waved them listlessly in front of his face. "Go by the cow camp and talk to him. If it's on the up and up he'll tell you."

"Tell me to mind my own business," Joyce said turning towards the door. "I know Jeff pretty well, too, Stumpy. He's no one to fool with. Either get him dead to rights or leave him plumb alone."

And while the deputy waited out sundown in the cool atmosphere of the Emerald Slipper Jeff rode into town, left his horse at the livery barn, got Al Waters out of his store and took him over to Matt Reynolds's office. There, he explained to them both about the shooting. Reynolds's pale gaze hung on Jeff's face but Waters was upset.

"Jeff—gawd—you can't go around shooting strangers. Listen; we're——"

"I didn't shoot him, Al, and he wasn't hurt. He's at Pacheco's; Antonio Garra saw him there this morning."

Matt Reynolds smiled. "Jeff," he said quietly, "Al and I met him."

Jeff looked dumb. "Met who?"

"The feller your rider shot the horse out from under." Matt said. "He's the Federal land appraiser from Raton."

For several long ticks of the clock on Reynolds's office wall absolute silence prevailed. The shooting faded into insignificance in Mordant's mind. He said: "The cattle; he saw us driving them—got a look at their brands—knows whose critters they are and now he's staying at Pacheco's." A rippling curse burst past his lips.

Al Waters was watching Matt. The tall, thin man had just the faintest wisp of a smile hovering around his blood-less lips. In a placating tone he said, "I think it's going to be all right. After I introduced him to Al I bought him a drink and had him in here for a little while. We talked —about land, values, re-appraisals—stuff like that."

34

Jeff recovered slowly. A thick pulse beat heavily in his throat. "The bribe?" he said.

Matt's chair creaked. He leaned forward, put both flesh-less arms on his desk. "I felt him out to-day, Jeff. He's coming back in tomorrow. We'll get down to dollars then." The pale eyes lost their irony. "That was a tomfool thing you did, though. I expect you know that."

"*I* didn't do it—didn't have any part of it. A trigger happy squirt did it and I fired him this morning before breakfast. All right," Jeff said, his voice gaining strength again. "It was crazy; I'll admit that; but it's past and what's important is the next step, which, as I see it, is this land agent."

Matt squinted his eyes. "There's something you're over-looking, Jeff. He saw you driving off Tres Cruz cattle. If he can be bought it won't amount to a hoot in hell. If he can't you'd better get those cattle back." The pale eyes bored in. "Why didn't you tell me you were planning something like that?"

"If it'd worked you'd have gone along, Matt."

The land dealer heard the warning dryness to the words and said no more. Jeff got up and threw them both a wooden nod and left the office. After he'd gone Al Waters lit a fat cigar and gazed steadily at Reynolds.

"He's too cussed reckless, Matt. He'll land us both in a peck of trouble."

But Matt didn't think so. "Nope," he replied. "Jeff's learnt a damned good lesson. He'll be more patient from here on, I think."

"Lord; I hope so. Now what?"

"See me tomorrow afternoon about this time, Al. By then I'll know where we stand with Donnellen." The bony face grew still. "And Al—I got a buyer for your third and my third. An all cash deal, on the barrelhead, when we've got title."

Waters rolled the cigar to the side of his mouth. "I thought we were going to lease to Mordant."

"Lease to the devil," Matt said, "when you can't do anything else. This offer I've got's for *three dollars an acre, cash!*"

Waters's cigar emitted a short burst of smoke. "How good's the buyer, Matt?"

"Plenty good. Big cattle syndicate from Nebraska; worth millions."

They sat gazing at one another for quite a long time, then Waters stood up and lost his worried expression. "Three dollars an acre, cash. Two dollars an acre profit on twenty thousand acres apiece. Matt; if worst came to worst you could hire a man killed for a twentieth of that, couldn't you?"

"Yes, you could. See you tomorrow afternoon."

When Waters was back outside he looked down the roadway half expecting to see Jeff Mordant riding out, but he was a half hour too late. Jeff was poking his way northwestward in sullen discomfort. The only sliver of satisfaction in him anywhere, was the memory of the things he'd said to Enos when he paid him off. Hard, threatening things of sufficient force to frighten the younger man clear out of the San Luis country.

But inwardly he blamed himself too. Riding through the dying day with a reddening sun gushing blood-light over the scorched earth he knew anger at himself. He'd doubted Enos from the start. Had watched his nerves turn raw on the trail. He lifted his head and the grey eyes were like wet iron. All right; he'd made a bad mistake. A bad one. But now it was over, past. The important thing was not to make another mistake. He drew rein on the hill under the unkempt oak and looked down at his cow camp. Two men down there in the cottonwood shade sweating beside a spindly little supper fire. Caleb and Garra. He pushed his horse down the slight incline and cool air rushed to meet him from the creek. It washed away his grimness.

After he'd turned his horse loose, piled his gear, Caleb was pouring a third tin cup of coffee and Garra was heaping a third tin plate with grease-coated venison steak. When Jeff came up they exchanged grunts, sat cross legged and ate. Several times Caleb slid sidelong glances at Jeff, but when the first man spoke it was Garra.

"Know who that feller is?"

"Yes, I know, and the worst thing Enos could've done was potshoot his damned horse."

Garra chewed a moment. "Enos is gone and that's that, ain't it?"

"Yeah. More coffee, Caleb."

Garra cut the grease in his throat with coffee, swishing it around in his mouth before swallowing it. Very methodically he wiped his plate clean with an unrooted tuft of grass. "I been over by Pacheco's looking around. Thinking they might be up to something. They were. The stranger came foggin' it back from the direction of town and the others got horses saddled and tied outside the corral. I left before they rode anywhere but——"

"How many saddled horses?"

"Four. Looks like Epifanio, Ramon, old Juan and the stranger are going ridin'."

A thoughtful crease deepened between Jeff's eyes. He finished eating in silence, made a cigarette and studied the lighted tip. When he rose Caleb got up also. Jeff looked over at him. "You two stay here just in case they're planning on paying my cow camp a visit. I'm going to ride out a ways and see which way they go." Garra came off his haunches with a questioning look on his face. Jeff saw it. "Don't worry; if they head this way I'll be ahead of them. They won't catch us asleep."

He saddled a fresh horse and rode southwest. The sun was gone but light remained. The temperature was still high in the eighties but without direct rays to buttress it the early evening was pleasant enough. He rode as far as a flinty rise, left his horse on the far side, squatted where he could see the distant ranch yard and smoked. Shadows made it difficult to see well and after a steady five minutes of squint-eyed staring Jeff was satisfied there were no saddled horses in the yard. That meant of course, that the Pachecos and the stranger—the Federal appraiser—had already gone.

Jeff swung his head slowly, Indian fashion, blocking in squares of country, seeking movement or dust. He found none. Very deliberately he turned completely around and looked towards his cow camp. The same; no movement, no dust of travellers. He stood up, deeply puzzled. They had either left hours ago, in which case he wouldn't be able to see any sign of them, or else they hadn't gone at all. He thought it must have been the former. If so, it meant they had a long way to go.

Realization came swiftly, then. They were going after the cattle, of course. He pinched out his cigarette, dropped it and bent a long, baleful stare at the ranch yard again. As he watched a rider swung around the barn on a fresh bay horse. Old Juan, the vaquero? It was too far to make out much more than movement. The rider disappeared on the south side of the barn and emerged going west. Jeff watched; thought one of the Pacheco crew had been delayed and was now hurrying to catch the others. With a mocking smile he went back to his own horse, swung up and paralleled the horseman. There was one way to discover what the Pachecos were up to. Follow the rider.

The shadows appeared, lean, furtive spots of shade on the east sides of little hills, rocks, trees. Jeff rode slowly past them and through them keeping lots of territory between himself and the rider he was pacing a half mile north-ward.

In the crystal distance the great shaggy old mountains loomed dimensionally larger, darker, stark and clear. They loomed so large distance was lost in their magnitude; they appeared miles closer than they were. An hour or so later their mighty shadows tumbled in brooding disarray over the range and Jeff wondered, looking into the gathering dusk, whether he might not lose his man after all. Until the rider reached the chaparral country there were no rocks to telegraph distance and route via horse shoes. The earth was spongy, it muffled sound. He meas-ured the distance to the flinty ground and knew instinc-tively the Pacheco rider would not hit gravel until long after dark.

Twisting a little in his saddle where the land dipped, he could see the rider, unhurrying, plodding steadily west, a shadow darker than the motionless shadows he moved through.

Well, there was one way; ride around the stranger, approach him head-on, stop him and ask where he was going. Nothing subtle about it but nothing particularly wrong with it either. He would have preferred to just trail him but darkness was closing in too fast, the rider travelling too slowly.

He lifted the horse into a smooth lope and bored ahead for about a half an hour, then swung a ways and cut back due east, mentally calculating his course to coincide with the other man's route. Once, he heard a horse blow it's nose. The animal wasn't more than twenty yards south of him but it was still a long quarter of a mile away. He angled so as to intercept the rider, was rewarded by the dull music of rein chains and spur rowels, reined up, made a cigarette and hung it in his mouth but didn't flick the match to it until the other rider saw him and jerked back suddenly, then he spoke, slitting his eyes, seeking recognition.

"Evenin' pardner. Ride on up."

His reins were looped, a match lay close to his thumbnail in the left hand, the right hand lay casually close to his gun-butt.

"It's Jeff Mordant—in case you can't see any better'n I can."

The stranger didn't move. A dull circle of whiteness showed a clean shaven face, the rest was lost in shapeless shadows. Jeff flicked the match, pinched down his eyes against the brilliance, inhaled, snapped the match in two, dropped it, and edged his horse towards the stranger with a cold smile.

"You act like I startled you, pardner."

When they were close Jeff lifted his left hand, drew in the reins and dropped them, staring into liquid black eyes, a face of cameo clarity; a woman's face. He was nonplussed just for a second. Of course—dammit— the men had ridden on . . . Garra had said something about a girl.

Neither of them spoke for a drawn out moment then Jeff slumped, lay his hands over the saddlehorn and studied her. He knew, from hearing it over the years, that some female relative of the Pachecos came to visit them each summer. Another pepper- . . . From deep within him a burst of shame swept up, night air cooled a warm glow in his cheeks.

"Well?" She said, without moving her eyes or blinking them.

"Well—good evening, ma'am. I—'you just out for an airing."

"Does it concern you?" She countered, and he noticed that one of her hands was gripping a loaded Spanish quirt with unnecessary force. He noticed other things too; she was beautiful. Small but full-bodied; lost glints of light hidden deeply within her jet black hair.

"No," he said slowly, "I reckon it doesn't. I thought maybe you were a Pacheco."

"Were you looking for them?"

He pursed his lips and didn't answer. She had the initiative, something he didn't like. "I wasn't looking for *you*." he said.

"Then there's nothing more to say," she said sharply and lifted her left hand, the one with the braided reins in it.

"Well," he said quickly, "there might be."

"What?"

"Is Epifanio at home?"

The black eyes bored into his face and after a moment's silence she said, "Mister Mordant—I think you know the Pachecos are not at home."

"How would *I* know?"

"How? Because you saw from the little hill you were watching the ranch from—before you trailed me."

Irritation surged up, made his face stormy in the gloom. He saw her eyes widen, the knuckles around the whip grow white and that irked him still more. In a flat way he said, "Lady; that quirt wouldn't help you—but you don't need it. You're plenty safe with me—like a rattler's safe." He took his hands off the horn and his horse's head came up, the beast took a tentative step, then another. He tore his eyes from her face and felt his back grow stiff as he moved past her. A low word followed after him when she spoke to her mount and Jeff rode a hundred feet before he twisted in the saddle to look back, and at the precise moment that he did her horse shied violently from a flushed jackrabbit and threw her. With a curse he whirled and spurred back. She was lying flat when he dismounted and knelt, eased an arm under her shoulders and raised her.

With the first white light across her face Lola Valdez's

beauty cut in under Jeff's heart like a knife. Without thinking he ran a rough palm over her cheek. At the touch she opened her eyes. For a second fear and astonishment looked up at him, then fury came and before Jeff could dodge she had struck him a fierce blow in the face. He caught her wrist and closed his fingers down around it like a vice. Anger made his voice unsteady.

"What the hell's wrong with you, lady?"

"What did you do, you—rustler, you?"

"Do? *I* didn't do anything. Your horse shied from a rabbit and dumped you." His mouth closed suddenly, the jaw set. "What did you call me?"

She moved away from his supporting arm and didn't reply. Standing up, facing him, she was easily eight inches shorter than he was. They stood like that a moment then she turned and started towards her horse. He watched her go, saw her brush one hand against the side of her head and guessed she'd been stunned. When she had her horse, was standing beside it, he walked up.

"I guess you heard me called a rustler somewhere, lady, and I expect one of the Pachecos said it."

She had the mane-hold and reins in her left hand, the saddle horn in her right when she looked up at him over her shoulder. "Anyone could have said it. You have that kind of a reputation, Mister Mordant." In the quickening moonlight she saw him as he was, a man, a fighter, a tall, bronze-faced predator standing tall in the environment that had whelped him, the same environment he had fought and kicked and buffaloed his way to the top in. A strong man made up of good and evil, courage and cruelty, the way God made all men; a mixture of honesty and wickedness, a tough, unrelenting man consumed with desires, passions, deep and fiercely burning ambitions.

He moved around beside her. She made no further move to mount and eventually dropped the hand from the horse's neck and faced him squarely. He felt the anger burn low, the indignation die, the lifelong tenseness go out of him as though drained out by the blackness of her look, the liquid softness with the iron-hardness lurking far back in the depths of her gaze.

"Whoever said that, Miss, is a liar," he said quietly.

"But you'd like to know who said it, wouldn't you; so you could hunt them down."

He shook his head at her. "No, I guess not," he said. "As long as *I* know it's a lie—why I suppose that's all that matters."

She looked mildly surprised. "I didn't expect you to say that." Before he said anything she spoke again. "Why did you drive the Tres Cruz cattle into the back country, Mister Mordant?"

"Why?" There was the plausible lie about them cluttering up JM range. Equally plausible was Caleb's remark about scrub Mex bulls breeding good JM Herefords.

"Yes, why?"

"It's a long story," he said evasively, unable to lie to her.

With a whirl she mounted the horse, sat looking down at him. "I imagine it is. It must be. Not only a long story but a very serious one as well; you wouldn't have shot a man's horse from under him if it wasn't a serious affair, would you?"

"I didn't shoot the cussed horse, lady. The man who did is gone. I fired him."

"That doesn't answer why the horse was shot, does it?" She had the initiative again. "But you aren't going to answer that, I know."

"You don't know———"

"Mister Mordant," she said, bending a little over the saddle horn, brushing aside what he'd been saying. "I think I know why you were out here tonight. I'll save you some riding—they went after the cattle."

He stood there with the moon flooding around him watching her lope back towards the Pacheco place, a muffled, spongy sound echoing the passage of her horse. When he went to his own animal, swung up and rode towards the cow camp chagrin rode with him. His cheek stung from the slap but his mind stung worse. She had out-guessed him at every turn and something else—something warm and painful lay heavy behind his belt.

Chapter Three

Jeff took a bath in the creek, rummaged through the wagon for clean clothes and put them on, caught, saddled, and mounted a horse and asked Garra what he had in mind for the day. The 'breed said there was reason to believe some JMs were drifting off the Reynolds lease; he thought maybe he and Caleb had better ride over and see. Jeff agreed it would be a good idea and rode away from the cow camp towards San Luis.

The world of smashing sunlight went unnoticed, little herds of cattle he passed were appraised from habit, and by the time he was on the outskirts of San Luis he had rubbed the cheek she'd slapped, twice.

At Waters's store he caught Al's attention long enough to jerk his head sideways, in the direction of Reynolds's office, then went over there himself, entered Matt's private room and dropped into a chair. The abstractor gazed at him pensively, and leaned back, bony hands clasped behind his head.

"What's up, Jeff?"

"I don't expect that land man's been in yet, has he?"

"Nope. I don't expect him until later."

Jeff's glance grew ironic. "He'll have to damned near fly to get here today, at all. He went after Pacheco's cattle with the old man, Ramon, and their Indian."

Reynolds's eyebrows went up. He said nothing.

"Listen, Matt; I've made one mistake after another in this thing. Chousing those cattle into the malpais country wasn't the first error."

"No? What was?"

"Forcing the grant up for re-appraisal."

Reynolds took his hands down from behind his head very slowly, in almost spastic jerkiness. He laid them palms down on the desk and stared at Jeff. "What do you mean?"

"I should've gone to old Pacheco, tried to buy the land first."

Reynolds looked perplexed. "What the hell's gotten into you, Jeff; you know doggoned well they'd never sell a foot of that grant. Those people never do."

"Nevertheless I should've tried to buy it instead of forcing them into losing it."

The diluted blue eyes were motionless. Gradually a faint sheen of antagonism showed in them. The bony face grew sharper. Reynolds made a short grunt and said, "By God; you've sure changed all of a sudden. What's wrong?"

"Nothing's wrong. I've just been thinking, is all."

"Well, by golly, Jeff—you ought to get over it."

Al Waters came in, shot a glance from one to the other and sank limply into a chair. In a slow and painfully clear tone Matt Reynolds said: "Jeff says he shouldn't have called out this re-appraisal, Al. Says he should've tried to buy the land from old Pacheco first."

Waters slewed his eyes to Jeff. His forehead creased into puzzled wonder, the eyebrows fell, lowering. "What's wrong, Jeff?"

"Nothing's wrong," Jeff answered irritably. He squirmed in his chair. "I rode in today to make a suggestion." He was looking at Matt. "Hold off on bribing this Federal man until I've had a talk with old Epifanio. I want to try and buy the land legally, first."

Waters shot a startled glance at Matt, who was regarding Jeff strangely.

"He might sell. Lord knows he doesn't need a fourth of the land he's got. If I can make him see———"

"Jeff," Matt said softly, "old Epifanio hates your guts. You know that don't you?"

"It isn't that bad."

"The hell it isn't. I've heard his kid talk about you. They've got no use for you at all. Now, listen, Jeff; you go out there and try to get that old feller to sell land to you and he'll more'n likely throw you off the place."

Jeff's eyes clouded with worry. Stubbornly he said, "Just the same, don't go to work on that Federal man until I've tried." His grey eyes lifted, hung on Matt Reynolds's face. "Savvy?"

Matt sat like a statue. Al Waters felt through his pockets for a cigar, lit it and squared around on his chair to face Jeff. "Jeff, the time's past for that. The land man's here, we got to buy him quick before old Pacheco smells a skunk and goes to work on him, himself."

Jeff wagged his head without looking at Waters. "No danger there. Pacheco doesn't have that kind of money. He couldn't bribe that feller unless he sold a lot of cattle— and quick."

"That's what I mean," Waters persisted. "He *could* sell 'em; raise the money, bribe this guy first and that'd leave us sucking the hind teat." Waters's voice changed pitch. "Listen, Jeff; we got this thing rolling pretty good now, for heaven's sake don't *you* throw rocks into the works."

Jeff turned his head a little, saw the intense anxiety on the merchant's face and felt surprise in a mild way. "You were the one who wasn't eager about this deal, remember?"

Waters made a sweeping gesture with one thick arm. "All right; maybe I was. That was before I got to thinking it over. I'm all for it now, hotter'n ever, so f'gosh sake don't ruin it."

"I'm not ruining it" Jeff said, "all I'm saying is give me a chance to get it done legally first."

Matt Reynolds leaned back in his chair again, most of the perplexity vanishing from his expression. "All right, Jeff," he said placatingly. "Go ahead. When are you going to see the old man?"

"Today some time. He won't be back until late afternoon or early evening though, so——"

"That's all right," Reynolds interrupted, in the same soothing tone. "Come see us tomorrow morning and let us know how you made out."

Jeff got up out of the chair. He looked a long second at Matt, then nodded and walked out of the office. When the sound of his spurs had faded Al Waters stood up. "What's wrong with him, Matt? Lord A'mighty—what'll happen to the other deal—the one with the Nebraska cattle syndicate—if he ruins this deal?"

"He won't ruin anything," Reynolds said. "I don't think he'll even get to open his mouth to old Pacheco. I happen to know the old man hates Jeff Mordant like only a greaser can hate. Jeff'll be lucky if he doesn't get shot, out there tonight." Matt shook his head. "The idiot. He isn't thinking like he usually does. Imagine—him going over to talk to Pacheco after the old man's just come back from a pretty uncomfortable trip after cattle Jeff pushed back into the malpais; why, Al, he'll be in a shooting state of mind, not a land-selling notion."

Waters fidgeted with his cigar, turned it over and over in his fingers. "Is that why you told him to go ahead and see Pacheco; because you thought he might get into a gun fight?"

Matt smiled. "It'd simplify the hell out of things, wouldn't it?"

Waters put the cigar back into his mouth. "Yes," he said. "But suppose there isn't any fight; suppose the old man refuses to sell?"

"Why then," Matt said, "it's up to you and me."

"Huh?"

"Remember what you said about being able to hire a man killed for one twentieth of what we stand to make out of this?"

Waters's cigar grew rigid. "Listen, Matt——"

"*You* listen. How long would it take you to make forty thousand dollars in the store? If you lived to be a hundred, Al, you'd no more make that kind of money in your business than I would in mine. For two thousand dollars we're still sitting in with a royal flush. If we don't spend the two thousand Jeff's going to spoil something we'll never get another crack at. Don't ask me why he's acting like this—I don't know. I *do* know it's got to be stopped one way or another or we both lose out on the chance of a lifetime."

Waters sank lower in the chair. "I don't like this, Matt. To be frank, I didn't like it too well when Mordant first came to me."

"You'd like forty thousand cash though, wouldn't you?"

Waters looked across the room. "Less one thousand— my share for having Mordant killed."

"Thirty-nine thousand cash then," Matt said pleasantly. "You'd like that, wouldn't you."

Waters nodded glumly. "I'd like that all right," he said.

"Then let me work out the rest of it."

"You'll have to. I don't know any gunmen."

Matt's smile reappeared. "I'll find us one. They're around like flies, when money's offered."

Waters left Reynolds's office. Out on the duckboards he paused to look at the traffic and saw Jeff come out of his store with several bundles. A powerful shock of fear flooded him. Suppose Jeff saw him; asked what he and Matt had discussed after he'd left them? He turned swiftly and ducked into the harness shop, bought a buggy whip he

49

had absolutely no use for and stood back in the shadows until he saw Jeff ride by.

Seeing the hard, set face of the cowman, Waters's fear came back. Abruptly he wished with unaccustomed violence he'd never listened to Jeff in the first place. The stories of Jeff's fierceness came back, lingered in his mind. He was afraid; very much afraid.

Jeff's face was screwed down against the reflected sunlight. It assumed a forbidding expression under the circumstances that didn't necessarily reflect any thoughts at all. Most men look grim when they're facing down the sunglare.

He rode as far as the cow camp clutching the bundles and when he topped out beside the old oak he saw three men sitting in the shade down below. Wariness came up. He rode down without looking at any of them, dumped the packages on the wagon seat, dismounted, turned his horse loose, dragged his saddle, bridle and blanket into the wagon's shade, then sauntered over where Garra and Caleb, and Deputy Marshal Burt Joyce waited.

"Howdy, Jeff."

He drained off a dipper full of water before he answered. "Howdy, Burt."

"Damned hot out."

Jeff dropped down in the shade, shot the deputy an amused, dry look, and said, "Sure is."

Joyce picked a tick off his neck, regarded it interestedly and crushed it between thumbnails. "Was over looking at a dead horse last night, Jeff. Went by here too late to visit."

Jeff saw Caleb and Garra watching him, removed his hat, ran some fingers through his hair and said, "How long've you been here, Burt?"

"Couple hours, I guess."

"What did Caleb and 'Tonio tell you?"

The deputy looked around. "About what, Jeff?"

"That damned black horse."

Joyce's eyes shone. "Nothing. They said they wouldn't talk to me about anything. All talking's left up to you."

Jeff built a cigarette and lit it. He gazed at Garra. "Thought you were going over to the Reynolds lease today?"

Garra jerked a thumb towards the deputy. "Seen him coming and thought it was you, so we came back."

Jeff nodded. "Well, Burt; I'll tell you about that black horse. I had a young buck working for me—fired him yesterday morning. He shot the horse."

"There was a man on it when he done it, wasn't there, Jeff?"

"Yes."

"Well—hell; which one was he aiming at?"

"I don't know. Maybe the man—only he hit the horse."

"Why? What was the feller doing he shouldn't have been doing?"

"Well," Jeff said, smoke interspersed with his words. "For one thing he was trespassing."

"That's not hardly good enough reason to shoot a man, is it?"

"No," Jeff said, "I suppose not. Listen, Burt—the feller who did the shooting's gone. He won't be back. The man wasn't hit and I'll pay for his horse. Is that fair enough?"

Burt's eyes squinted at the ground. In a soft drawl he said, "I suppose so, Jeff. 'Thing is, I'm not sure this feller looks at it quite like that. He's pretty sore about it. 'Told me he was just watching you fellers driving Tres Cruz critters and one of you threw down on him." Joyce's eyes lifted, swung, hung on Jeff's face, saw the tight, unpleasant look settling there. "Mind telling me why you were driving Pacheco's cattle?"

"Yeah, Burt," Jeff said, sitting up straighter, "I mind. I run JM's range the way I think it ought to be run. As

long as I don't break any laws it's none of your business—
or Stumpy's—how I run it."

"It'll get serious if you go to potshootin' travellers
though, Jeff."

Jeff stood up. "It might," he said, "but you'd better
wait until I hit one."

Burt got up stiffly, slapped dust off his britches. "In case
you want to see that feller who owned the black horse, he's
staying at Pacheco's. *Adios.*"

Garra got up, went to the water bucket, dipped a drink
and downed it slowly, watching the deputy marshal ride
up the knoll towards the oak tree. He flung the residue
from the bottom of the dipper when Joyce dipped from
sight on the far side, dug a tobacco sack and went to work
over a cigarette.

Caleb blew his nose lustily between two fingers and
went towards the creek. Jeff cocked an eye at Garra. "What
did he have on his mind—if anything?"

"The cattle drive, like he said. Wanted to find out
where we drove 'em and why so far. I told him to see you.
He didn't act too worried over the black horse."

Jeff propped his head up. "What a damn fool play that
was. Except for that shooting all this trouble wouldn't have
turned up."

Garra tilted his head, squinted at the sun. "Yeah," he
said absently. "It's too late to ride the Reynolds lease today.
Anything else you want us to do?"

"No," Jeff said. "Ride that tomorrow."

Caleb came out of the willows dripping water from his
hands and face. Garra moved towards some cards on a
saddle blanket. "Game of stud?" he said. Caleb nodded,
glancing down at Jeff who got to his feet. "How about
you, Jeff?"

"No; I've got a little riding to do."

He took two of the bundles with him to the creek.

Garra and Caleb could hear him taking another bath. They both looked up, around, then at one another in surprise; two baths in one day!

Dressed in a new white shirt, stiff new levis, Jeff emerged from the willows, caught up a horse, studied the lowering sun a moment, missed the wide glances shot his way by his riders, saddled up and rode across the creek and in a southwesterly direction from the cow camp. There was no urgency but he had that feeling just the same.

The sun was a punctured balloon atop the jagged fingers of stone far to the west. The range still writhed with heat but a promise of coolness came intermittently as he rode. Before he got to the flinty swell he'd watched the ranch from the day before, he bored a long look westward, seeking dust, signs of a cattle drive. There was something hazy a long way off but the glare made it nearly impossible to define. If it was Pacheco he'd be hours getting back. If it wasn't, it didn't matter. He wanted to see the old man; talk to him about the land. It wasn't much of a hope but he clung to the wish to try it. And if Pacheco didn't sell?

He pushed his horse down off the flinty lip, down the gradual slope to the creeping shadows below, a short mile from the buildings. If he didn't sell . . . The thick, surging ambition flooded up, sparked a burning cruelty, made Jeff's face draw tight and harsh. If he didn't sell, there was the other way.

In that frame of mind he approached the buildings. In his heart was a ruthlessness that wouldn't die. A man doesn't work like a slave for ten, fifteen years, to give up when he's within grasp of his greatest ambition. If Pacheco didn't sell, he'd *take* the land. Had to have it. Ten years from now—five even—a cowman on leased land or free-graze would be ploughed under by squatters.

The ache behind his belt began quite unexpectedly. He thought of Lola Valdez. Freeze the Pachecos out and there'd be hatred in her black eyes as deep as the night, as lasting as forever.

He watched the house move closer. It was silent, deserted looking in the richness of ancient shadows. Remained that way until he was clop, clopping two steps ahead of his echo across the bare ground to the edge of that patio; then he saw her. Sitting with her back to a gnarled oak, head up, watching him like a statue. He off-saddled, dropped the reins and stepped up on to the smooth stones.

"Good evening, ma'm."

For a moment she considered him in silence, then she said. "They aren't back yet, Mister Mordant—but perhaps you know about that."

He moved easily into the shade, made no move towards one of the benches, stood ramrod-straight twenty feet across the patio from her. "I guess it took longer than you thought —is that it?"

In a bleak way she said, "What did you do after you left me last night?"

"Why; I went back to my camp and bedded down."

"And this morning? You didn't send men after them —anything like that."

He saw the tightness of her mouth, the fear in her eyes, and understood. "No'm; you're worrying unnecessarily. Nothing's happened to them. It's quite a ride. They couldn't get back with the cattle until late tonight." He saw a little of the grimness go out of her expression. "I could go after them."

"You are naïve, Mister Mordant. I think they would kill you on sight, by this time."

He went closer realizing she wasn't going to ask him to be seated. Hunkering on the edge of a little bench he tossed his hat on the stone floor, unconsciously ran fingers through his chestnut hair and looked over at her.

"I shouldn't have done that, should I?"

54

Startled, she said, "You *are* naïve; you do things on the spur of the moment and are sorry afterwards."

"I wasn't sorry until—yesterday."

The black gaze was briefly puzzled, then he saw a hard glaze come over it; almost a repugnance. "If you've come to apologise, see my uncle."

His head bobbed up and down. "You're Lola Valdez, aren't you?"

"I am."

"Strange we've never met before. You've been coming to visit the Pachecos for a long time. I've heard of you."

"There was no reason for us to meet, just as there was no reason last night—except for your spying."

He leaned back. Through his shirt a coolness crept into his shoulders from the adobe wall. "Mind if I smoke?" he asked.

"Do you intend to stay that long?"

He looked down at the tobacco sack, concentrated on creating a cigarette, lit it and looked back at her. There was something close to amusement in his glance. "Ma'm; you sure work hard at being disagreeable."

"With you I have no reason to be otherwise."

He exhaled, watching the way the reddening sun burnished her hair where it came filagreed through the oak leaves. "Kind of rude, too," he said.

She started to snap it up but closed her mouth, pursed her lips instead and said nothing. The dark look was more eloquent than anything she could have said anyway.

"That slap last night . . . I was helping you, not hurting you, ma'm."

A slight ruefulness appeared temporarily and vanished. She hugged her silence.

He turned his face and watched the soft shadows fall. Smoke trickled up from the cigarette in his hand, broke under his jaw and curled backwards along the wall.

"Peaceful spot." She made no reply and he looked at her again. "Tell me something; why do the Pachecos hate me?"

That was too good an opportunity. Her eyes flashed at him. "It would be better to ask why they shouldn't. For years you have driven their cattle off the range——"

"Off JM range, ma'm."

"There is enough grass for all—except a range hog."

"It isn't the grass," he said, then stopped speaking, arranged his words and said, slowly. "I'll tell you my side of it. You've already heard the Pacheco side. I came into this country with very little money. That was a long time ago. I brought a few head of good Hereford cattle with me. Down the years I've worked hard breeding up my cattle and securing my range. I was a kid when I came in here, now I'm a shade past thirty. I don't aim to waste those years by having my cows fetch scrub Mex calves out of Pacheco's speckled, olive-hipped, buffalo-humped, longhorn bulls. Does that sound reasonable to you?"

"Why don't you keep your cattle away from my uncle's bulls, then?"

He bent a pitying look on her. "Ma'm," he answered patiently. "When a cow's bulling she'll walk fifty miles to find a bull. I've got two riders besides myself and fifteen hundred cows. Figure the answer out for yourself." He crushed out the cigarette and tossed it away. "*I* think I've been doggoned tolerant. Where I was raised the ranchers had another way of handling those scrub Mex bulls. They'd ride out five or ten at a time and alter them—make steers out of them."

"You would have no right to do that," she said quickly.

"I don't think you come from cow country," he said. "If you did you'd understand that legal rights and range rights aren't always the same. If ranchers who own scrub bulls won't get rid of them what chance have other cow-

56

men got who've spent years and lots of money up-grading their cow herds?"

She was silent. He watched her, seeing the reflected turmoil of her thoughts. After a while he said, "That's my side of it, but there's more. The Pacheco's have got eighty thousand acres of range and about five hundred head of scrub cattle. Five thousand acres would be sufficient for their needs."

"Who are you to say what other people need," she flared at him.

"A cowman," he answered simply. "I know this range. Know what it takes to run a cow and calf. Miss Valdez— do you think there is *any* right on my side?"

"I—don't know."

"That's not an honest answer, we both know it. I've been frank and honest with you."

"Perhaps, but then, as you've said, I'm not from cattle country. I live down at Raton. My people are merchants. Only my uncle and cousin are ranchers." She looked a little past him. "But I've liked this country since I was a little girl. That's why I come up here each summer."

"It gets pretty hot," Jeff said.

"What country doesn't this time of year?"

"And there are bad neighbours, rustlers, in it."

"That wasn't necessary, Mister Mordant."

"Jeff."

"Mister Mordant!"

He lapsed into pleasant silence. The shadows were longer now, thick and substantial looking. "Miss Valdez—what is it about these oldtimers that keeps them from raising good cattle? Those cussed slab-sided Mex critters don't carry five hundred pounds of beef on them but they eat just as much grass as good cattle do."

"That," she said emphatically, "is something you couldn't understand."

He looked at her. "Couldn't I? Because they are Spanish cattle. The kind Spaniards have always run in the Southwest. Sentiment, ma'm; just plain sentiment.

"It is deeper than that, Mister Mordant."

"I know. It goes back to the times when this country belonged to the Spaniards. Seeing the same homes, the same vaqueros—Indians, always—the same country, and finally the same cattle, creates an illusion of sameness; the illusion that Spain and Spaniards still rule here. But they don't Miss Valdez. That's all long past. I know Spaniards in Texas who have fine Hereford herds, irrigated haylands, American riders. They're progressive. Tell me something; your father's a merchant. If he still sold Spanish pikes and leather britches could he stay in business?"

"I won't argue it," she said. "But my Uncle Epifanio is an old man. What he does with the rest of his life is no one's business but his own." The black eyes met Jeff's grey ones. The storminess was gone. "He can't start over again. At eighty-six one lives in the past; he is no exception. If his cattle are scrubs as you say, it is because they belong to a time when all cattle were scrubs. They won't change I don't suppose and my uncle *can't* change."

Jeff considered this. "And does his dislike of me go as deep? I mean—is it because I'm progressive—and Yanqui —that he has no use for me?"

"Not exactly. Spaniards aren't that way. I can't say as much for many Yanquis, as you call them. In your case it is the things you've done. I've heard some of the stories, too. You have been fighting too long, possibly, but you are cruel, Mister Mordant. You are hard and in most ways ruthless. Like driving my uncle's cattle so far at this time of year. It wasn't necessary."

The land, he said to himself. The land. Steer it around to the land. "Miss Valdez, have you met the man who is staying here with your uncle?"

58

The dark eyes looked up quickly. "Mister Donnellen? Yes, of course. He is the man whose horse you shot."

"Is he a rancher?"

"He hasn't said and we haven't asked."

Jeff sighed inwardly. "But he's angry about the horse?"

"Of course. Wouldn't you be?"

"I guess so. That's one reason why I rode over here this evening. Pay for the horse and talk to your uncle—about something else."

Tartly she said, "You picked a bad time, I think."

Reynolds had thought the same thing. Jeff looked towards the west. If the dusk wasn't so thick he was sure that by now he'd have been able to see dust.

"Mister Mordant?"

"Yes'm?"

"I'm sorry. I apologise for slapping you."

His tongue got suddenly quite thick, clove to the roof of his mouth. Eventually he said, "Were you trying to find them, last night?"

"No; I was just riding. It was cool, a pleasant time to ride." She looked steadily at him. "Why did you follow me?"

He could feel colour beating into his face. The shadows hid it however. "Well—to tell you the truth I wanted to know whether your kinsmen were going after their cattle, or whether I'd have to bring them back myself."

The dark eyes didn't waver. "A change of heart?"

"Not exactly. I had good reason to want them back."

She made a small gesture with her hands. "What is this all about?"

"What; the cattle?"

"No; everything. The cattle, yes, but there's more to it. Not just the dislike between you and my uncle. That's existed for years, I know. But who is Mr. Donnellen, why does he ask so many questions and volunteer nothing about

59

himself? Why is he so interested in the Pacheco grant, and you."

"Is he?"

"Yes. And more than that, even." She leaned a little, looking at him in the dusk with compelling earnestness. "Is something going to happen? I have that feeling." She straightened up quickly, seemed to remember something for her expression resumed its reserved look, its coolness, a shade of the antagonism again. "I shouldn't ask you though, should I; my uncle's enemy."

Quite suddenly he stood up. Down the soft night came tired lowing, it lingered bugle-like, then died away. He stood listening but no repetition came. He turned slightly to look at her, bent, took up his hat and held it by one curled edge. "Miss Valdez; you've heard why I'm the way I am. You also must realise now that I haven't done any of the other things I could do, to get rid of the annoyance of your uncle's Tres Cruz cattle. I guess, if you wanted, you could think the thing right down to bedrock and it'd come out that your uncle's the old way and I'm the new way. I don't want to bother him but, dammit all, I get pretty sick of being bothered by him. There's another thing too," he said recklessly, ignoring the warning that trilled in his mind. "There's the grant; your uncle's got four times as much land as he needs to run what stock he has or ever will have."

His words stopped. She had risen, was facing him across the patio and even in the gloom with the first light of the full moon drenching the range, filtering vaguely through the leaves, he could see the way her eyes had widened, her mouth had partly opened as though she was listening to something from within.

"Of course," she said softly, finally. "The land, I didn't think of it before. That's it, isn't it, Mister Mordant? You want the Pacheco grant."

60

The warning rang louder. This time he considered it. Stood in silence watching her and the soft light grew bolder, stronger, touched the deep shadows without entirely dispelling them, showed their faces, shadowed their eyes.

He saw the dislike seep into her expression and felt powerless to stop it. He watched her stiffen, the abated antagonism, defiance, return, and still he didn't answer.

"Why did you drive my uncle's cattle away? I'll tell you. So he wouldn't be here for a few days, perhaps. You had a plan in mind for those days, didn't you?" Her heavy lower lip grew thinner, flatter. "For a little while I thought possibly, you had some right on your side. You're clever, Mister Mordant."

When she stopped speaking the sound of cattle lowing in the middle distance came again, closer. Once he heard a man's hoarse call.

"I didn't lie to you," he said suddenly, doggedly, and from his own words drew small satisfaction. "All right; that's the other thing I rode over here to talk to your uncle about."

"But you knew he wouldn't be here."

He nodded. "Yes, I knew."

"Then you are lying now, Mister Mordant."

"No. I—had an idea. I wanted *you* to help me—to ask him if he would sell part of his land."

"Me?" She said in a rising way, really surprised.

"Yes." The hard grey eyes were steady. "I guess I never did have much hope you'd do it, but I thought you might at least tell your uncle what I wanted."

"I will," she said firmly. "I'll tell him everything you've said here tonight."

"Listen, Miss Valdez," his words fell flatly into the night. "Trouble's coming for your uncle. He can avert it by selling some of his land——"

"To you, of course."

"Yes, to me. I'm not the only one who wants it but at least if he sells it to me it'll still be open range."

She made a brittle laugh. "What else can you make of land like this but open range, Mister Mordant?"

"Homesteads," he said succinctly. "Cut it up into little patches with wire fencing around it." She said nothing and he went on. "I won't fence it and if your uncle'll upgrade his cattle I won't even object to his running with mine."

"That's generous," she said, "I'm sure my uncle will understand just how generous." She turned away, walked swiftly towards the patio door, into the house beyond and left him standing there with night sounds crowding in around him.

He remained rooted for several minutes. No lamp-glow came from the house. He left the patio, crossed to his horse, swung up and threw a long look at the dark patio. Thought that a little of himself remained there. A man's call floated through the paleness, he turned and rode at a slow walk back the way he had come.

Reynolds and Al Waters would be fit to be tied if they'd heard him telling her about the land. He'd handled it all wrong; aside from angering her he'd left the story to be given her uncle second-hand.

With a tumult of jumbled emotions within, he finally reined up, made a cigarette, lit it, cupped the match up close to his face and inhaled, snapped the match, blew smoke out and resumed his slow way northward.

What made him handle the thing so badly? Why had he ever thought she might be prevailed upon to aid him? But for a while, there on the patio in the dusk, in the soft, mellow evening, she'd softened a little. If he hadn't mentioned the grant she might have. . . . He drew in a great lungful of smoke. Too fast; he'd rushed things, pushed her too fast. Tried to accomplish in one sitting what should have been done over several visits.

The white shirt glowed in the moonwashed night. The little red end of his cigarette was an infinitesimal beacon that could be seen a long way off. Around him the night was silent, deep, soft-running with the expelled breath of parched earth and drying grass. Within his mind was the recollection of a hauntingly beautiful face, bitter black eyes and a gently moulded silhouette. To a hard man such things come doubly strong; carry with them a devastation which hardness can't fight.

Well, like his first and second mistakes, it was done. He was almost fatalistic about it. Superstitiously fatalistic. For some unfathomable reason he was apparently destined to do everything wrong in this affair. The calling out of a re-appraisal in the first place. An action dictated by his hardness and ambition exclusively. Enos's shot, in the second place. He had no control over that but it boomeranged to his discredit nonetheless, and now this—making the girl hate him more than ever. Tipping his hand in such a way that Epifanio Pacheco would hear of it with hatred making the words drip defiance of his offer. All wrong.

But worst, she loathed him and it had come at a moment when she'd been at least reconciled to believing all wrong wasn't on his side, for a few moments at least.

He looped the reins around the horn and let the horse pick his way across the open country south of the flinty hillock, and sucked on the cigarette and didn't see four riders sitting up there on the ridge watching his white shirt and glowing cigarette end.

Chapter Four

They stopped him with a word when he was close to the lip of the hill. Ordered him to come all the way and keep his hands in plain sight. Ramon's litheness was what he saw first, then Juan the old vaquero, darker than old brass even in the moonglow. The big stranger, hawk-like, fierce looking, stonily silent and unmoving, and lastly, the reed-like thinness of old Epifanio. It had been his voice that stung into the night like taut wire, words full of menace, of scarcely controlled wrath.

"Mordant . . ."

"That's close enough," Ramon said. He bent a little, flicked Jeff's gun out, tossed it down. Murder was like black oil in his eyes. Ramon straightened in his saddle, sat still, looking into Jeff's face. The old Indian, gnarled, bent, was ashen with fatigue. Old Epifanio's lips were bluish in the moonlight, his eyes like dry coals. When he spoke the words fell like steel balls striking glass.

"Señor Donnellen—this is the man responsible for your black horse's killing. He is also responsible for the condition of my cattle."

Donnellen's sharp features turned slightly, his gaze hung steadily upon Jeff. In a thick tone of voice he said, "That horse was an old companion of mine, Mordant. If you'd had a reason to kill him it might be a little different. You had none."

Jeff's smooth face was blank, his eyes unwavering. In the shadowed well below his cheekbones, jaw muscles rippled. "The man who shot your horse had no orders from me to do it. I fired him for doing it and I'll pay whatever you think he was worth. That was a bad mistake; I didn't do it but I'm responsible enough to make it good. What was he worth?"

"I wouldn't have sold him, Mordant," the larger man said. "How do you make that up to me?"

Jeff hesitated over his answer. Anger was filling his veins. If Donnellen held him up on the price there was nothing he could do about it. He nodded brusquely. "Put a price on him. I don't like to be robbed but I'm committed this time."

Donnellen wagged his head lazily. "I won't hold you up; I don't need the money. What I want is satisfaction, Mordant."

"All right. I've got over a hundred head of good horses. You can take your pick."

Donnellen's eyes showed no interest. "I'll buy my own replacement," he said. "As far as you're concerned I think you've got a lesson coming." Donnellen closed his left hand down over the saddle horn, swung his right foot free and eased his weight into the left stirrup. "Get down, Mordant. I've heard you're a tiger."

Jeff watched Donnellen dismount. For a moment he looked into the faces of the other three horsemen. There was cold hostility in three sets of black eyes. He dismounted, went around his horse's head and dropped his reins. Donnellen had his back turned, he handed his reins to Juan and straightened around. Easily three inches taller than Jeff, he out-weighed him by more than thirty pounds. Jeff was not a small man but he was lean, snake-hipped, sinewy rather than bulging with muscle. Stamina, endurance, opposed to crushing, overpowering force. Epifanio's saddle creaked. The old man was bending forward a little, eyes like drops of oil. When he spoke the hard edge of triumph was in his voice.

"Mordant—my cattle are in bad shape. Some we had to leave, their feet were too sore to move. They lost a lot of weight. Why did you do that to me? Not because my animals were on JM range—don't tell me that—it's deeper. Why?"

Jeff looked over at the old man. "I can't talk and fight too. I'll answer you when this is over—maybe."

Donnellen smiled. "Good thing you put that 'maybe' in there."

Jeff matched his grin with one just as humourless. "I didn't mean I wouldn't be able to answer, I meant I might tell him why, and I might not, it depends on what conclusions I come to." He jutted his chin at Donnellen's holstered gun. "Pretty heavy, isn't it?"

Donnellen's smile grew fixed, unpleasant. "Don't worry about that, Mordant. Move away from your horse."

Jeff moved, turned his back on the Pachecos thinking as much as they disliked him they wouldn't interfere. Donnellen, as Lola had observed, walked flat on his feet. He crunched across the flinty soil towards Jeff, both big arms up, fists out. "This'll teach you not to potshoot a man's horse, Mordant. Maybe it'll teach you something else, too. Quit being hog of the range."

Jeff saw the first blow coming, had no trouble side-stepping it; he back-pedalled from two more and turned sideways, moving around Donnellen when the big man loosed a barrage of flailing fists only one of which landed, high on Jeff's right arm as he whirled away.

As Donnellen came around his breath whistled and Jeff lashed out with a stinging, overhand right that popped like a rotten melon against Donnellen's cheek. The big man stepped back, completed his turn and rocked forward to start after Jeff again. A vicious left, low and blasting fast slammed into Donnellen's stomach. The big man stopped dead. His mouth slammed closed. Jeff hurled in a chopping

66

blow and followed it up by closing, arms pumping like pistons. Donnellen's head snapped back once, blood flew from his nose. A terrific slash smashed into his jaw, he took another backward step and Jeff pummelled him at will. Donnellen kept his feet until a hurled handful of knuckles burst up against his forehead, directly between his eyes. From that moment the fight was over.

Donnellen rocked, weaved, and Jeff's breath sounded like a dull saw cutting dry wood. It rasped, broke and came almost in sobs. His bony hands were everywhere. Battering at Donnellen's face, his midriff, his chest, stomach, then he stepped back a second, fired everything he had into another blow to the forehead and Donnellen went down like a large tree. Jeff stepped over him, took his pistol, dropped it into his own holster and turned, straightening, to face the Pachecos. Ramon looked stunned. Epifanio's face was masked with blankness that didn't quite conceal the gorge of disappointment. Juan, the withered old Indian, looked awed. He blinked his eyes.

"Pacheco," Jeff said with an effort to control his breathing, "I left a message for you with Miss Valdez." He looked at Ramon and the Indian a moment, thoughtfully, then jerked his head sideways at them. "You two go on. Ride towards home." When Ramon made no move to lift his reins Jeff said. "Your dad'll be perfectly safe. I just want to talk to him for a few minutes; now go on."

Ramon was obdurate and Jeff turned to his father. "I can make him go but it'd be cleaner if you asked him to."

"What is it you want with me?" Old Pacheco asked.

"Talk, that's all. Just five minutes' talk."

"Go on, Ramon. You too, Juan."

Jeff waited until they were going down the slope then he moved back to his horse, mounted, gazed briefly at the limp form of Cliff Donnellen, and said, "Pacheco; I didn't realise until tonight how useless an idea I had, was. I knew you didn't like me but that it went this deep———"

"Shouldn't it? My cattle———"

"All right; I shouldn't have done that. You aren't the first one to point that out to me. I'll pay whatever you think is fair for the weight loss and the trouble I caused you."

Epifanio blinked. For a while Jeff didn't think he was going to speak at all then he said, "Why? Why did you drive them off? Why do you now offer to pay?"

"I made a mistake." A tincture of bitterness crept into his voice. "I've paid for my mistakes one way or another all my life. I'll pay for this one."

Epifanio's gaze grew round, perplexed. "Why did you drive them; let me ask you that."

"I'll answer that later, maybe. First let's settle the amount I owe you."

"I don't understand you, Mordant."

Jeff smiled thinly, nodding at Donnellen's lumpy silhouette on the ground. "Neither does he. Don't try; just tell me what I've cost you."

The old man's forehead crinkled into deep furrows, the cold anger in his glance was replaced by something else. Something compounded of suspicion, distrust, pure wonder. "I have no idea. It is a smaller matter, perhaps. The cattle will recover. The rest of it . . ."

Jeff grew impatient. "All right; think it over, figure out a price and let me know. Another thing: I realise I'm not handling this right and it's just come to me that I'm a cowman pure and simple, not a very good schemer."

"I don't follow———"

"Pacheco," Jeff said bluntly, "will you sell me part of your grant?"

"My grant?" Epifanio said. "Sell part of it—to you—to anyone? No! A thousand times no."

"Listen to me a minute. I'm responsible for this—I'll

tell you that before someone else does—but your grant's been ordered up for re-appraisal." Jeff pointed down at Donnellen. "Your guest there—he's the Federal appraiser sent here from Raton to figure out how much land you actually need to run your Mex cattle on. If his figure comes out lower than your eighty thousand acres, you lose it. It's put up for auction. Do you understand?"

Pacheco sat like a stone, stunned. After a moment he said: "And you have the nerve to tell me you did this? I will kill——" His shaking hand stopped short, hovered over the pistol-butt. Jeff's gun bored its one-eyed stare over the swells of the saddle.

"Don't, Pacheco. Move your hand away. That's better." The brittleness of his voice carried in the night. "I'll tell you something else. If that land goes into public domain homesteaders'll get it. They'll put up fences, plough the range, run more scrub cattle. Pacheco; hate me to hell and back if you want to, but don't let clodhoppers get that land. I'll keep it open-range if you sell it to me."

In a husky voice the old man said, "Mordant; I'd see it ruined—see fences and homesteaders all over it before I'd sell you a foot of it."

"You'd ruin yourself, Pacheco."

The old eyes were alight. Pacheco nodded quickly. "I'd do that too, if it would ruin you."

Jeff felt the waves of hatred come out of the old man, beat up against him like hot air. Slowly he holstered his gun, lifted his reins and rode away.

The warm night, pale, iridescent, followed him with a great shadow all the way to the cow camp. A hunched shadow—his own. When he turned his horse loose and lay on his blanket a host of thoughts, swollen with disgust at himself, kept sleep away.

He hadn't expected to succeed, perhaps, but he'd wanted to try. Beneath the effort, behind the motive, he knew, was a subconscious urge to talk to Lola Valdez again. Try to make her see his side just a little, not hate him quite so much. Had he succeeded? He laughed in a wolf-bark sort of way.

For a long time he lay like that then very slowly he held up both hands, studied the battered knuckles bitterly, sat up and made a cigarette. When the smoke was cascading from his mouth he looked up at the moon, aloof, alone, and asked himself where the hardness, the ruthlessness was, she insisted he possessed. And he knew the answer to that if she didn't. It was gone. Age hadn't mellowed it, softened him, and he knew that too. *She'd* done it; made him something he'd never been before; a man against force. How? He blew smoke skyward. With black eyes and creamy complexion. With fire and passion—yes, even with her hatred of him—because he was fighting to keep her *from* hating him; he wasn't fighting for the Pacheco land now.

With a rough curse he lay back again, smoked until the cigarette burnt his fingers then tried to close his mind against Lola, against the entire affair, and couldn't.

The old man would break himself to injure Jeff Mordant. *That* was hatred; he'd never known it like that, himself. Well, but the old man couldn't fight him any other way. He ran crooked fingers through the nest of his hair and sat up again. Fight an eighty-six year old man, a skinny kid—and a girl. Gawd but you're brave, Jeff, he told himself. And range-wise too. So damned range-wise everyone including Lola Valdez knows by now what you've done—turned loose on the old man—Reynolds, Al Waters, a re-appraisal that can't miss carving the guts and heart out of the Pacheco grant. Played the entire hand like cards were something new; like a downy-cheeked kid would play them. Like Enos would play them.

With teeth locked down tightly against fury, he leapt up, stood broodingly glaring at the night a moment, then went after a horse, saddled up and rode for San Luis without a backward glance.

He rode slowly, lost in a maze of bleak thoughts, more disgusted at himself than at anyone else and when he saw the first pale smear of dawn in the east he wasn't far from San Luis. Whipped the damned land appraiser too . . . Matt and Waters would throw a fit. Thoroughly bungled everything. He rode into town from the north, angled towards the livery barn, put up his horse and went out into the deserted, silent roadway and teetered on the plankwalk. One thing to do; just one thing: Stop Matt and Reynolds and someway, somehow, get rid of that land man. Reynolds and Waters wouldn't be hard to handle. Waters wasn't more than lukewarm until yesterday and Matt—well—Matt could be bought off. That left Donnellen. The grey eyes grew cold. Bribe him to clear out, forget the grant—if he wouldn't there was another way. He looked at his swollen hands again. Big Donnellen; big and tough, full of war talk . . . Like cutting down a big sapling in a windstorm; he would do it again but Donnellen had to clear out without condemning the grant.

He went to the Chinaman's for a breakfast of eggs and bacon, three cups of oily black coffee and another cigarette. Afterwards he sat, back to the counter, ignoring those who entered and recognised him, watching Reynolds's office until the skeletal owner came jerking along, then he threw down the cigarette and went out into the morning, crossed the road and followed Matt inside.

"Jeff! What got you out so early?" A long look at Jeff's face and the abstractor said, with misgiving plain in his voice. "Not another cattle drive?"

Jeff didn't speak until they were in Matt's office. He kicked the door closed and dropped into the chair before Reynolds's desk. "Listen Matt; you and Al've got your hopes built up about this re-appraisal; well forget it. Whatever you two are out I'll make good."

Reynolds's face tightened, his mouth set, and weak coloured eyes came to rest without moving, almost without life they were so still and motionless. "What the hell are you talking about, Jeff? We can't stop just like that."

"Yes we can and we're going to."

"You started this ball rolling, y'know."

"All right, so I did. I'm going to stop it, too."

Matt's face underwent a change. There was something menacing in it. "Jeff; just exactly what the hell's gotten into you the last couple of days? Yesterday you were off your feed too. Listen; if something's wrong tell me and I'll get it untangled for you. If you think Al and I're taking too much land, whatever it is———"

"I'll tell you this much, Matt. I've done some pretty mean things getting up where I am, but that doesn't mean I've got to go on doing them. As far as the re-appraisal's concerned—no dice."

Reynolds subsided thoughtfully then he said, "Al won't like this either." He paused a moment longer. "Jeff; spit it out—what's gotten into you?"

"Turning over a new leaf, you can call it, Matt." He stood up. "Find out from Al what the damage is and let me know; I'll pay it." He left the office and Matt Reynolds watched him go. For several minutes the thin man remained behind his desk. When he rose and started for the door, finally, his legs moved with brittle haste.

At Waters's store he entered the owner's office and threw a grim nod at the sturdily built man who looked up at him. "Al; Jeff was just in to see me." In sharp sentences he recounted what Jeff had said. Waters listened and swore. When he would have spoken Reynolds silenced him with a motion. "Like I said yesterday, I've no idea what's wrong with him but I don't intend to be cut off like this either." He stopped speaking. The silence was full of meaning.

Waters's face mirrored anxiety and greed. He mumbled something under his breath then raised his head and said, "There's no choice, is there?"

"None."

"Then you'll find the gunman?"

"I'll find him today if I can. There are ways to find those men."

"Dammit," Waters said anxiously. "For less money I wouldn't sit in it at all."

Reynolds smiled bleakly. "Give me a thousand dollars," he said.

Waters sat a moment, then went to his safe got the money and handed it to Reynolds without a word. Reynolds stood up, looked at the bills and pocketed them. "This puts you in right up to the neck," he said, still wearing the unpleasant smile.

Waters sank back into his chair. "Are you sure these Nebraska people are ready to buy?"

"Pretty sure. They wired me last night. I wired back for them to send someone out here to look the land over."

"But you haven't seen the Federal man again, have you?"

"I'll see him today. If he doesn't come in I'll go out and find him."

But Reynolds didn't have to. Donnellen rode into San Luis an hour after Jeff had ridden out. He met Reynolds in the abstract company's outer office, was invited into the private office.

Matt saw the bruises, surmised Donnellen had fallen from a horse and overlooked them. The big man sat, sprawled, and there was banked fury in the depths of his eyes. Matt saw it and was wary. It took him over an hour to steer the conversation where he wanted it and very abruptly Donnellen gave him the opening he sought with a harsh sentence.

"Tell me if I've guessed wrong, Reynolds," he said. "You want the Pacheco grant condemned."

"I do," Matt said frankly.

"What's it worth to you?"

"The grant?"

"No; condemnation."

Matt leaned back, clasped hands behind his head and felt good. "Two thousand dollars, cash."

"Double it," Donnellen said flatly.

Matt nodded imperturbably. "All right; four thousand dollars, cash."

Donnellen began to twist up a cigeratte. He spoke without looking up from it. "What's your interest? You didn't call out the re-appraisal, Mordant did." He lit the cigarette and stared at Reynolds. "Has Mordant an interest in this?"

"None at all," Matt said softly. "Why?"

"Because if he did have I'd turn you down cold. He and I had a fight last night."

Matt sat transfixed. The bruises stood out clearer of a sudden. He cursed Jeff inwardly and dropped his hands to his lap. "A fight? What about?"

"Pacheco's cattle. I think he drove them off to make it look worse than it is for old Pacheco. I called him on it. We had a fight. I wish I'd shot the dirty whelp."

Matt's eyes flickered. "Why didn't you?"

"Didn't get the chance. Reynolds; what're you going to do with the land, if I condemn most of it and you get it?"

"Re-sell it," Matt said truthfully.

"Does Mordant know this?"

"Of course not. He'd raise hell if he did. That's open-range out there, he's had the run of it for nearly fifteen years—ten years anyway. Newcomers wouldn't be welcome."

Donnellen looked darkly pleased. "It'd be better if homesteaders got it, I think. They'd put up fences, plough the land. That'd hurt Mordant worse than anything."

Matt was shaking his head. "I don't think so. Mordant's scairt out his share of settlers. I'd sell it to big cattlemen from out of the country. The first time he threw a long loop with them they'd kill him. That's how they work. It'd be a lot more certain than having a bunch of clodhoppers mixed in."

"Someone'll kill him," Donnellen said. "Yeah; I think you're right at that. Cattlemen'll do it quicker than squatters." He smoked a moment. "I'd give a hundred to see him killed."

Matt smiled. "I'd give *two thousand* to *have* him killed," he said.

Donnellen's fiery glance swept upwards, clung to Matt's face. He appeared shaken out of his sullen anger. Cigarette smoke spiralled upwards from the hard curve of his mouth. "Four thousand for the condemnation—how much land you want condemned?"

Matt drew in a long breath and said, "Sixty thousand acres. Can you justify that?"

"Easy," Donnellen said. "The old man's only got about five hundred head of Longhorns. Sixty thousand acres taken from the grant leaves him twenty thousand acres; a hell of a lot more'n he needs. All right—give me the four thousand dollars."

Matt made no move to rise from his desk. "Do you want the other two thousand?" he asked softly.

Donnellen exhaled, removed the cigarette from his mouth and regarded it for a moment. "Yes," he said finally. "That job'll be a pleasure."

Matt took out the thousand Al Waters had given him,

laid it on the desk, unlocked a desk drawer, removed an iron box of small size, opened it with a heavy key, and counted out another thousand, locked the box and put it away. "There's two thousand. You'll get the four thousand when you show me that sixty thousand acres of the Pacheco grant have been condemned. Is that agreeable?"

Donnellen looked at the money then reached for it. "I reckon," he said. He counted it, wadded it into his pocket and stood up. "Reynolds; does anyone else know about this?"

"Not a soul," Matt said glibly.

"Then if it leaks out it's got to come from you, hasn't it?"

Matt understood the implication. "It won't leak out," he said. "Don't worry about that."

"I'm not worrying, Reynolds, but if it does *you'd* better start worrying."

Matt didn't appear bothered. After the Federal man left he sat lost in thought. Thirty thousand acres apiece was much better than twenty thousand acres, split three ways. Sixty thousand dollars profit for he and Al Waters on a thirty thousand investment for each of them. And Mordant—That was luck—He gradually lost his rapt look and his eyes clouded over. What in the devil was wrong with Mordant? Why had he picked a fight with the very man he'd schemed to have condemn part of the Pacheco grant? What was behind his sudden and complete reversal?

Matt Reynolds couldn't imagine but Jeff had no illusions, himself. Lola Valdez . . . He thought of her as he approached the cow camp, found it deserted and off-saddled, drank deeply at the water bucket and stood erect in the sunlight with the sound of a ridden horse coming to him from the west. When the rider appeared he knew it wasn't Garra or Caleb. For a moment he thought it might be one of the Pachecos or Donnellen. It turned out to be Burt Joyce, dripping sweat and dry looking around the mouth.

The deputy dismounted near the water bucket, dipped up a cool drink, downed it, had a second one and hung the dipper back on its nail before he turned and said, "Howdy."

Jeff felt annoyance coming up. "Still looking at that dead horse, Burt?"

Joyce made a wry face. "Can't get very close to him any more. Carcasses don't last long this time of year."

Jeff walked over into the shade and hunkered. The lawman followed over in a shambling way, dropped down and sighed.

"Hot enough to roast eggs," he said. "Been looking at the Tres Cruz cattle. They've had a lot of abuse lately."

Jeff remained silent thinking Epifanio had sworn out a complaint against him and Burt was there to serve it.

The deputy eyed him casually. "You seen 'em, Jeff?"

"Not lately."

"Not since you drove 'em off, eh? Well; they're back. Old Epifanio and his crew brought them back. Pretty tucked up and footsore." Joyce plucked a stem of curled grass. "Rough when men get to the place where they fight one another using dumb animals as ammunition, I think. Only ones get hurt are the animals."

"Listen, Burt——"

"I'm not here for trouble," Joyce went on quietly. "The old man hasn't said anything about you driving 'em off."

"What are you here for?"

Joyce put the grass stem between his teeth and looked at the weathered old wagon. "Oh; just on my way back to town. Thought I'd drop by and cadge some dinner."

Jeff was exasperated, not hungry, but he got up and went

towards the tailgate of the wagon. Over his shoulder he said, "Stir up the fire and I'll see what we can hustle."

They worked in silence, hardly looking at one another. They ate the same way, in a kind of undeclared hostility. When the deputy was through eating, smoking, regarding Jeff speculatively, the cowman doused the fire with a dipper full of water and sat down again. Steam hissed and some huge, shiny flies swooped in hungrily for the scraps.

"I was over at Pacheco's," Burt Joyce said. "They're pretty upset about something, Jeff."

The grey eyes grew pensive, watchful. "Didn't they tell you what it was?"

"No. In fact Ramon stayed outside with me. I could hear the old man and that girl arguing inside. Sounded like a pretty cussed hot argument too, but it was in Spanish."

"You can understand Spanish," Jeff stated.

Joyce grinned crookedly. "Not when they're talkin' it like shooting a gatling gun I can't." His eyes looked amused but they bored too, studying Jeff. "That girl's enough t'take a man's breath away. Don't see how Ramon stands it."

"She's his cousin," Jeff said warmly.

The deputy shook his head. "Don't make a damn," he said. "If I had a relation looked like that—well—I don't know what I'd do."

"Talk," Jeff said tartly. "Like you're doing now. Shooting off your mouth."

But Joyce's amused look atrophied. Interest replaced it. He sat gazing over at Jeff for several silent moments, then he shrugged. "What d'you suppose has got the Pachecos so upset?"

"Oh hell," Jeff snorted at him. "If you're hinting about those damned cattle spit it out."

"I wasn't—especially. Is that it?"

"I don't know; probably. Was the stranger around?"

"Nope. Reckon he lit out for town pretty early." A pause. "Jeff?"

Sensing the change in Joyce's voice Jeff looked up. "Yeah?"

"You wouldn't want to help me unravel this trouble would you?"

The grey eyes remained steady. "No," Jeff said.

Joyce sighed, rocked forward, unwound his legs and stood up. "I didn't think you would," he said, looking down and standing in front of Jeff. "Just a thought, anyway. By the way; seen the stranger about his horse yet?"

"I saw him last night. In fact—you'll hear about it anyway—we had a fight."

"Guns?"

"Fists. Went over to see Epifanio. On the way back rode into the old man, Ramon, their Indian, and this big feller."

Joyce's eyes narrowed. "You don't look very cut up," he said.

"Wasn't much to it," Jeff said. "He's got size but so's a range bull."

Joyce nodded. It had happened before between Jeff Mordant and larger men. "Over the horse, huh?"

"Partly that. Partly because he was sore over having to ride so far after Pacheco's cattle."

"Hmmm. He's working for the old man now?"

"I don't know, maybe."

"Did you offer to pay for the horse?"

"Sure. Offered to pay or replace him. Told him he could have his pick from my cavvy. He wouldn't have any part of either."

"And called you—and you whipped him."

"That was about it," Jeff said, looking up from the ground at the lawman.

"You think that ended it?"

Jeff shrugged. "I don't know. Don't know the man well enough to say. I kind of doubt it though; he's a vindictive looking cuss. Big and sort of hatchet-faced."

Joyce fished around in a shirt pocket for his tobacco sack. "Jeff; you've got the dangdest knack for making enemies of anyone I ever saw." He held the sack by its little yellow cord looking downward. "Golly; it's like you want folks to be sore at you."

Jeff leaned back gazing upward at the standing man. "Burt; I did my damndest to make it right to that feller. I went over to Pacheco's to try and talk sense into the old man. I didn't have any luck either way, wound up in a brawl, even made a new enemy. Maybe it does look like I'm trying to make folks dislike me but I'm not."

"Go back a few years, Jeff." Joyce had the cigarette going. It bobbed up and down from between his lips as he spoke. "Go back ten years and more. There were squatters. Later on there were legal homesteaders. Fights in town. Bad blood with a few of the other cattlemen." He waved his hand. "You never ducked around a corner to avoid a fight in your life, I don't think. Leastways if you did I never heard of it."

Jeff's irritation returned. "If ducking fights means being liked, why then I guess I'll always make enemies," he said. "When I was a kid we called duckers cowards."

"You're not a kid any more. Anyway you don't have to run from it when someone's really out for you, but you sure Lord don't have to take up everything that's said about you either. There'll always be folks who talk about other folks; most folks ignore 'em. Not you—you want to hunt them down and fight 'em. Well; it's your way, Jeff, but someday you'll get it. I'm not very old but I've seen it happen that way a hundred times, believe me."

Jeff said, "Through, Burt?"

The deputy nodded.

"See you in town."

Joyce nodded, shifted his feet a little and looked over where his horse stood drowsing in the shade. "Yeah," he said absently. "Sometimes I talk too much. All right, Jeff. Thanks for the chow and s'long." He walked as far as the wagon, passed it, long legs swinging easily, spurs making faint music, the brilliant sunlight catching him when he left the shade by the wagon, and out of nowhere came the smashing report of a carbine, high, sharp, stingingly clear.

Jeff spun off the ground, took several big strides towards the wagon and saw Burt Joyce lying face down in the trampled grass. Joyce's spurs vibrated, his toes stubbed the dirt and Jeff turned very carefully squinting up towards the shaggy oak on the knoll. The echo died quickly with a high, singing sound but nothing moved. Jeff went along the wagon as far as the seat, pressed in close, groped for a carbine, grasped it's warm barrel and drew it out. He looked once more for movement, saw none, crossed to the deputy and went down on one knee facing the direction of the shot. There wasn't a sound.

Reluctantly he laid the carbine aside, grasped Joyce's shoulder and rolled him over. A freshet of blood gushed from Joyce's mouth, obscured most of his face and shocked Jeff briefly. Very methodically he removed his shirt, wiped the blood away and saw the unnatural way Joyce's jaw hung. He plugged the gaping hole in Joyce's right cheek and the jagged tear opposite it, went to the creek, soaked the shirt in cool water and worked in savage silence until he'd fashioned a bandage. By then Joyce's face was blue, his eyes dry-hot looking, half conscious, tortured. Jeff stood up and sweat ran off him. He felt helpless before the wounded man's agony and turned when he heard riders coming.

Garra dismounted first, mouth slack, eyes fastened to

81

the wounded deputy. He said nothing but his expression spoke volumes, all eloquent, all mistaken. When Caleb walked up stiffly, stood staring down, his adam's apple worked in a retching way before his pale glance went to Jeff and hung there.

"What happened; he try to shoot you?"

Jeff straightened. "Me? *I* didn't shoot him."

Garra looked unconvinced. He shrugged. "Who did?"

"Somebody from up near the oak."

They both gazed up at the knoll. Garra ran his reins through his fingers a moment then swung up and rode slowly towards the knoll. Anger arose in Jeff as he watched the 'breed's progress. He turned to Caleb.

"Ride to San Luis, fetch a doctor and a spring-wagon or a buggy. He's in bad shape."

"Looks like it," Caleb said dryly. "In the head? He's bluer'n a Yankee's pants."

"Through the jaw. Ride, dammit!"

When Garra came back his face was curled into a lowering scowl. He dismounted and held up his palm. A brass casing lay on it. Jeff took the thing, smelled it and pocketed it.

"What kind of tracks?"

"Shod horse, but it'll be dark pretty quick, Jeff." The muddy eyes were troubled. "You two alone—this ain't going t'look good, you know that don't you?"

Irritably Jeff spurned the innuendo. "I sent Caleb to town for a doctor and a wagon, but 'Tonio, I've got a better idea. We can't leave him lying here. Ride over to Pacheco's, tell them what happened and ask if they'll send for him and keep him at their place until the doc arrives."

Garra nodded and turned away.

Jeff watched him lope across the sun scorched range with worry like an ulcer eating into him. Garra and Caleb had thought he'd shot Joyce. If Joyce died . . . He went over and knelt beside the injured man. Big black flies were gorging on the black blood. He shooed them away, saw that unconsciousness had returned and hunkered there for hours, fear growing with each bubbling breath, ragged, uneven, Deputy Marshal Burt Joyce drew.

Chapter Five

When the wagon came from Tres Cruz Antonio Garra rode beside it. Old Epifanio, thin, erect, rode far ahead with Ramon. The Indian drove the wagon and ignored Garra as stolidly as though he didn't exist. Jeff saw Epifanio and Ramon first. None of them nodded when the Spaniards dismounted, walked over and peered down under the rude shelter Jeff had made above Burt Joyce. Ramon said something harsh in Spanish. His father made no reply but straightened and looked at Jeff.

"You shot him?"

"No—dammit. He was ambushed by someone up on that hill. Where's the wagon?"

"It's coming," Epifanio replied, gazing at the wounded man again. "This is hard to believe. He visited with us earlier."

"So he told me," Jeff said. He heard the wagon, watched its plodding team, moved impatiently. "Give me a hand. We'll use these bedrolls for———"

"No need," Ramon said coldly. "The wagon has a mattress in it."

When old Juan set the foot-brake the five of them lifted Burt Joyce, eased him into the wagon, shielded him from the sun and started back. Jeff had to catch a horse, saddle up and hasten after them. Garra rode beside him, rust coloured face sombre, mouth locked tightly.

At the ranch Jeff caught a glimpse of Lola after they'd carried Joyce inside, put him to bed in a cool, dark bedroom. She moved past him as though he were invisible. He hesitated then went out to the patio, sank on to a bench in the shade and made a cigarette. Garra came out, hunkered nearby, waiting, as raffish looking as ever.

"That big feller ain't here," Garra said irrelevantly.

Jeff looked at the 'breed briefly, then ignored him. What of it? What difference did that make? A moment later he said, "'Tonio; you'd better ride to town and fetch back the marshal. Caleb probably won't think of that; he's after a sawbones. If you see him tell him to forget the wagon—we've got Joyce at Tres Cruz and from the looks of him I don't think he ought to be moved for a while."

"If ever," Garra said, standing up, squinting out at the shimmering late afternoon. "All right. Shall I come back here or wait for you at camp?"

"At camp."

Because Antonio Garra was the only moving thing as far as Jeff could see he watched him out of sight, then Epifanio came outside and stood in the shade saying nothing. Jeff looked around at him.

"I suppose Burt's got enemies, like all of us—too bad."

Pacheco leaned against the wall of the house. "Would his enemies know he was going to your camp?" he asked.

Jeff understood and brushed aside Pacheco's suspicions. "Would I shoot him in my own camp?" he countered. "I had nothing against Burt."

"Nothing you couldn't whip him over, anyway," Pacheco said dryly. "You two are about the same size, the same build. You whipped Donnellen, a much larger man. Burt wouldn't be hard for you to handle—with fists."

Jeff looked at his hands, felt futility seeping through him. "No point in arguing," he said. "You think he forced me to use a gun on him. Dammit, Pacheco; why would I use a *carbine* at that distance?"

"I have no idea. Circumstances sometimes . . ."

"Circumstances my foot. Burt wore a pistol and so did I. If we'd gun-fought it would have been with pistols."

Pacheco fell silent and Jeff's mind went dully over the shooting. In the cool silence the ranchyard was thick with strange peacefulness. Jeff felt it even as his mind picked at the details of Joyce's shooting and as such things sometimes happen, something Epifanio had said assumed quiet and looming importance. "You two are about the same size; the same build . . ."

Very softly Jeff said: "Pacheco; I think it was a mistake."

The black eyes swung down, lingered. Pacheco kept silent.

"Whoever that was meant to shoot me, not Burt."

"That's possible," Pacheco said. "Burt is well liked."

Jeff stood up, his face twisting ironically at the older man. "And I'm not," he said. "All right—I'm not!" He left the patio as shadows crept out into the yard and the scarlet sun loosed streamers from the rim of the far-away mountains. Went down to the barn in an aimless way and ended up leaning on the smooth, ancient corral poles lost in thought.

Who? Who had tried to kill him? Bitterly he admitted the truth of Epifanio Pacheco's remark. He had enemies; wasn't well liked, but who hated him badly enough to ambush him? Names, faces, drifted in and out of his consciousness, some clear and vivid, some obscured by time, half forgotten. Which one? He turned, leaned his shoulders on the poles and stared across the cooling yard with its mauve shadows.

Tiredness welled up. Mental weariness; a sort of sadness made up of loneliness, self-reproach, knowledge that he'd been fighting so long, so ruthlessly, that he now stood alone and disliked although at the top of the heap of San Luis

Valley cowmen. A hollow triumph and along the way he'd made an enemy who now wanted to kill him.

When the sun was gone and the yard swam in universal gloom he made a cigarette, smoked it slowly, heard someone crossing from the house and looked indifferently at the swaying silhouette.

She stopped ten feet from him and a strong scent of carbolic acid preceded her. "I thought you had gone," she said tonelessly.

The cigarette drooped from his lips. "I'm sorry to disappoint you. I've been thinking; forgot the time."

"You'd have much to think of, wouldn't you," she said.

"You too? Would you believe I didn't shoot him if I swore it?"

Her answer was slow in coming. "Swore it on what? What do you swear your oaths upon?"

With abrupt and reckless bitterness he said: "On the one thing I want above all other things—your friendship."

She moved abruptly towards the barn. With three great strides he blocked her way. "And since I can't have that —I reckon it doesn't matter whether I shot him or not, does it?"

"I—you are impossible to understand. Impossible."

He said: "I've heard that before and the answer's the same. Don't try." Blood pounded in his head, beat low in his throat, made the pulse in the side of his neck swell and ebb in the darkness. "Women want men they can mould —rule—don't they?"

She stood stone-still looking up at him, saying nothing, half-afraid, half fascinated by the coldness in his face.

"Why did I tell you about the re-appraisal? To give us a common ground; a way to see each other, not as enemies. To give you a way to guide me, Lola . . ." He broke off, staring at her. "Good Lord," he said very softly, very intently. "I think I know who shot Burt and why . . ."

They were close, staring at one another. A thin, gaunt fingerling of moonlight fell across the corral, made bony shadows at their feet.

"Reynolds—Waters . . ."

"Who are they?"

He seemed momentarily to have forgotten her, ran a hand over the bristle of his jaw.

"Outlaws, perhaps?"

His gaze focused on her face. "Come over here; over by the corral. I want to think out loud. You can tell me if it sounds reasonable."

He started at the beginning and told her the entire story. The moonlight spread, glowed, softened each hard contour of the old barn. Mellowed the baked breadth of earth and when he finished speaking Lola Valdez wasn't looking at him. Her face was turned towards the house where lamp glow, rich and golden, tumbled from the windows, spread in little pools on the old stone patio.

"And if you are right," she finally said, "your evil is causing another man to suffer—perhaps die."

"Is he dying?" The words were troubled and sharp.

"Who knows? He is very low." She turned and looked at him. "Why are you like this? Why do you want an old man's land? You control more land than anyone needs. Why can't you live like other people—in peace?"

"I want to," he said.

She looked down. "There's blood on your shirt."

He looked at it, darker than ink, stiff in the moonlight. "You think I'm responsible whether I shot him or not, don't you?"

"Aren't you? If what you think about Reynolds and Waters is true—aren't you responsible for his shooting?"

He answered slowly. "I suppose so."

"Can you see yourself as my uncle and cousin—and others—see you? Ruining an old man, robbing his son, causing pain and suffering, perhaps an innocent man's death —the misery of others I've heard about? I know; you're wealthy. You have hundreds of fine cattle, miles of range. You've worked hard—like an executioner—getting where you are, and people hate you—hate you—want to kill you. Do you like that?"

He watched the way sincerity made her dark eyes glow and without answering stooped, picked up two pebbles, tossed one out into the yard and where it landed a small echo came back. He toyed with the other stone and said. "It got thrown out there, didn't it, and if it's to keep from getting kicked it's got to roll by itself, hasn't it? Look," he held up the other stone for her to see. "Catch it." She did and he nodded at her hand. "The other one's protected. There's someone to guide it. Do you understand?"

She looked down at the pebble with a minute frown. "A parable," she said. "I prefer plain words."

"As long as you hold that stone your warmth will keep it alive. You'll influence it, Lola. The other one is cold. It has only itself to rely on. One judgment is never as good as two and as long as it lies out there being kicked it is without warmth. It is cold and hard and will remain that way."

In the unseen distance a buggy's rattling brought Lola's head up swiftly. Jeff turned to listen. It would be the men from San Luis. Perhaps Garra and Caleb were with them. He turned back slowly and saw her piquant profile. Saw how her small fist was still closed around the pebble and got the impression that she was only half listening to the men coming down the night.

"Do you understand what I meant?" he asked.

Without looking at him she said, "I understand," and started quite suddenly towards the house. Over her shoulder she said, "I hope you find your warmth and guidance some-day. Before it is too late."

Disappointment flooded him. With no need for it he made a cigarette, lit it and forced his attention to stay on the swaying top-buggy that came noisily into the yard minutes later. There was a small group of horsemen around it. In the corral shadows they didn't see him. He waited until they were tied up before the house and sought out Caleb and Antonio Garra, left with the horses.

"Well?"

Garra's muddy eyes swivelled. Without a greeting he said, "The marshal brought couple fellers with him."

"And the doctor?"

Caleb grunted. "Yeh."

"Do they want me?"

Garra avoided a direct answer. "I said you'd be at the cow camp."

Jeff watched the dark face. "They think I did it?"

"There was some talk like that," Caleb said.

Jeff nodded. "All right. Let's go back."

The three of them rode due north from Pacheco's, then angled across JM range to the rolling country where the wagon stood, ghostly still, haunted looking under the big moon.

Garra and Caleb were hungry. Jeff had no appetite. He listened to them while lying back on his blanket and stared moodily at the sky. His thoughts of Lola and the desultory rattle of his riders, words intermingled in his mind. ". . . Grant wanted to know who knew he was at our camp . . ." She'd said she understood—hoped he'd find his warmth. ". . . Said I could've picked up that shell-casing any-where . . ." And the way she'd held the pebble, her face turned away from him; but she'd stayed, listened, talked to him. ". . . And Doc said if anyone was shot in your cow-camp it shouldn't be Burt Joyce." And she'd said he was ruining an old man, robbing his son, causing pain, suffering, perhaps an innocent man's death.

Without speaking Jeff got up, shook himself and walked past the wagon where his horse was, brought the animal in close, scooped up the saddle, slapped down the blanket and threw the hull across the animal's back. Antonio and Caleb had ceased speaking; sat motionless and cross-legged watching him. He stepped up, swung east and said: "I'll be in San Luis if they come looking for me."

Caleb cleared his throat, spat, and spoke quietly to Garra. "What in tarnation's come *over* him the last few days, anyway? Used to be easy to figure him out—now he's like a perfect stranger."

"This shootin'," Garra said indifferently.

"Naw; before that even. I———"

"Quit worrying about it and eat. I'm going around in circles too, but so long as he pays me I'll stick around and t'hell with figuring things out."

As Jeff rode away his thoughts shaped up. If Joyce had been shot as a result of mistaken identity, there was reason to believe the would-be killer was a hired gunman, a stranger, and if this were so, the most recent people he'd crossed were Al Waters and Matt Reynolds. And that made sense for neither of them, especially Matt, was in favour of having Jeff spoil the land-grab. Waters wasn't the type to hire a killer and Matt would steer clear of the actual shooting, himself. But, where Waters would shrink from hiring him killed he knew Matt Reynolds would have no qualms if the motive was strong enough.

And the first thing to do was stay away from strangers until he knew who the assassin was. The second thing was to get it out of Waters and Reynolds—if they were behind the attempted murder—who the drygulcher was. The third thing, of course, was to take care of the killer one way or another before he got another crack at Jeff.

He rode down the night with a restless irony in him. He was fighting now to defend the very thing he'd sought to destroy and he was despised by both factions. He rode alone against both sides and an unknown killer. And there was the Federal man. Something had to be done about him. Riding, he thought, if he came out of this alive it would be a miracle. Three sets of known enemies; only the Lord knew how many unknown ones, against him. The sense of loneliness returned and the still, brooding night enhanced it.

Before he rode into San Luis some of the inner harshness was lined into his face. If there was to be a killing; if gunmen were to be hired, Jeff Mordant wasn't a poor man or a quitter. He'd never avoided a fight in his life nor hired a gunman, but if he had to fight with hired guns and dollars, he had enough of one to hire the other!

San Luis lay bathed in quiet moonlight. The hour was late—or early—and a new day was not far off. With no thought of irregularity he rode to Al Waters's home first because it was closest, tied up and rolled his knuckles across the door several times. A dog barked next door. Across the road a smaller dog added his clamour. Waters came to the door with a lamp held high, a swollen face, and unpleasantness in his expression. Jeff shouldered past him into the room, shoved his hat back and stood wide-legged.

"Who'd you hire to shoot me, Al?"

The suddenness of it cleared Waters's mind like a dagger of ice. He stared, mouth slack. "What! What did you say? Have you been drinking, Jeff?"

"No, I haven't been drinking. Who is he?"

"Who?"

"Damn you, quit stalling. Who is the feller you hired to bushwack me?"

"I didn't hire anyone to kill you," Waters said thinly.

His nostrils quivered. "You must be drunk; why would I hire anyone to kill you?"

Jeff swore inwardly. Because Waters's house had been the first he'd come to he'd gone to it. He should've seen Matt first and knew it now. Without another word he left and Waters stood in the doorway, still clutching the lamp, staring after him.

More dogs were barking now. Jeff swung into the saddle and rode through several rutted back roads to Reynolds's place and tied up and, although it took considerable beating to rouse the householder, when Reynolds came to the door, strangely enough he was fully dressed although it was close to three o'clock. Fully dressed and with a cigar between his teeth.

"Well! Howdy, Jeff. Come in."

Jeff entered, smelt tobacco smoke and was turning towards Reynolds when the thin man jerked his head and started past. "Come on out back in the kitchen. I was just having a cup of java." As he walked, Reynolds talked. "What's on your mind? Too much moonlight to sleep?" In the kitchen he made a jerky motion towards a chair across the table from him, cleared away a soiled cup and laid out a fresh one. "Too bad about Burt, wasn't it?"

"Yeah."

Jeff watched the sinews writhe under Reynolds's skin when he poured coffee. In the same genially conversational tone Reynolds went on speaking. "They tell me Stumpy was fit to be tied."

"Is that so?" Jeff said. "Who do they think shot Burt?"

Reynolds set the pot aside, sank down and shrugged. "Lots of gossip, you know." The bland eyes raised. "I heard you were there when he got it."

"I was there all right. I wasn't sixty feet away when he went down."

"Hummm; didn't you *see* anything?"

"Not a thing. The drygulcher was up on the knoll by the old oak. It's all open ground from the camp to the knoll. I didn't go up there but Garra did, later. He found an ejected shell and some tracks, but that's all."

Reynolds made a clucking sound. "That's one of the risks of Burt's job. Stumpy's too, for that matter. Lawmen make a lot of enemies. Nine out of ten wouldn't have the sand to drygulch them but that tenth feller . . ." Another shrug, a small smile. "Not too good a shot though, from what I've heard. Is Burt dead yet?"

"He wasn't when I left Pacheco's."

Reynolds's eyebrows climbed. "Is that where he is?"

"Yeah; too badly hurt to haul him all the way to San Luis in a wagon. Say, Matt——"

"Who took him over there?"

"I sent word from the cow camp. The Pachecos sent a wagon."

In a dirty ashtray were two cigar butts. A soiled cup and saucer were on the sink where Reynolds had put them. Unusual time of the night to entertain guests. Jeff lounged in his chair thinking and when the silence was deepest he spoke, gazing steadily at Matt.

"Who was he, Matt?"

"Huh? What?"

"Who was the ambusher?" A dark scowl at Matt's puzzled look. "Who'd you hire to kill me? No—don't lie. I want his name. I came here get it—or you."

Reynolds's nonchalance crystallised into something brassy, something hard and wary. It showed in his bony face and in the depths of his unmoving glance. There was no surprise in his voice when he answered.

"I don't know what you're talking about."

"That's the first lie," Jeff said. "You know exactly what I'm talking about. That slug wasn't meant for Burt Joyce, it was meant for me. From that knoll your gunman thought

94

Burt was me. You know, Matt, your drygulcher made two mistakes. The first one was when he tried a head shot. The second was when he didn't make sure of his man."

Jeff sounded almost bland. He felt no anger. Too many hours had passed. "He's a stranger in the country or he'd have recognised Burt. Who is he?"

Matt didn't answer and with sudden, stunning force, *Jeff knew*. It must have showed on his face because Reynolds sat forward on his chair, staring. His left hand lay relaxed near the cup; he was unmoving and silent.

Jeff's hands lay in his lap. He moved them only to push against the table and stand up. "You made a bad mistake, Matt. Stand up. That's it—now walk ahead of me to the door." At the front of the house Jeff bent, plucked Matt's gun out, punched out the loads and tossed the weapon into the geranium bed. In thoughtful silence he stood hipshot, relaxed.

"There're all kinds of fools in the world, Matt," he said, "but I think the biggest fools are the greedy ones." His mouth pulled up a little in iron mirth. "I was one, so I know. They always make mistakes. Greed blinds men, doesn't it."

"Something's wrong with you, Jeff," Matt finally said, very softly. "You been acting strange for a week or so. Listen——"

"*You* listen: There's nothing wrong with me at all. I've changed some notions I've had, that's all. You haven't changed any of yours and more'n likely never will. For some reason you're more set on getting that grant than ever. Set enough to hire me killed. Don't deny it, Matt." The steely eyes were unblinking but not hard. If anything they were condescending, almost pitying. "You won't get an acre of it, Matt. Not one damned acre."

"Jeff, for gawd's sake, listen. You're all wrong. As for

95

the grant—man—be reasonable; be smart like you've been up to now. It's riches for three of us."

Jeff's iron smile widened a little. "For two of you, Matt. Maybe for just one of you, but I know this—you never intended for me to have a cut. Burt's shooting—the way it was done—convinced me of that."

"You're wrong, Jeff."

"No, I'm not. Quit lying. You want it this way—all right—but remember, Matt, shooting's a business that two work at. I ought to bust you in two right now but I'm going to give you a chance to drop the Pacheco grant business first. Forget it; do like I said, tell me what I owe you for the bother and forget it." He started to turn away. "You know where you can find me—at the cow camp. Send word what I owe you."

He left Reynolds casting a razor-like shadow and rode through the silent, moonlit town as far as the Emerald Slipper Hotel, left his horse and entered through the saloon annexe, awakened a drowsing night clerk and smiled into his puffy face.

"You've got a man staying here named Donnellen, haven't you.

"Well; he's staying here tonight, yes. Upstairs room——"

"What time did he come in tonight?"

"Tonight? About an hour ago, I'd guess."

"Where's his horse?"

"Livery barn, I reckon. We got no facilities for——"

"Thanks."

At the barn a night man was reading by the smoky, gusty light of a coal-oil lamp. He looked up when Jeff entered, threw him a short nod.

"Which stall's Donnellen's horse in?"

"Humph," the man grunted, getting up. "Come on; I'll show you."

The animal was bone dry and drowsing. Jeff jutted his chin at gear hanging from a hook. "Is this Donnellen's stuff?"

"Yeah; saddle, blanket, bridle, gun."

Without speaking Jeff drew out the carbine, walked to the rear of the barn, fired it, ejected the spent casing and dropped it into his shirt pocket. The liveryman stood dumbfounded, jarred wide awake by the gun's smashing explosion. Several windows rattled open, some awakened dogs barked. Jeff put the carbine back into the boot and flipped a silver dollar at the nighthawk.

"Want to make five more?"

The night man looked uneasy and Jeff thumbed back his hat, leaned against the stall door. "It's perfectly legal, pardner. All you have to do is say you shot at a coyote with your own gun. Say nothing about me firing Donnellen's carbine. Well?"

"I dunno."

Jeff counted out five silver dollars, reached forward and dropped them into the night man's shirt pocket and turned away without speaking.

He rode back through the small hour chill and a short distance from the knoll above the cow camp stopped long enough to flick a match and study the bullet casing. The firing-pin had struck at the extreme upper edge of the soft-cap. There were no scratches or marks left by the pin, indicating the gun had seen considerable use. The off-centre position of the firing-pin, then, was all he had.

He rode on into camp, turned his horse out, piled his gear and feeling relieved if not totally satisfied with his thoughts, was confident he knew who Burt Joyce's ambusher was. He lay down with his arms under his head and watched the stars until sleep came.

Antonio Garra plucking at his sleeve awakened him. He

looked up, sat up, rubbed his eyes and spat. Garra was hunkering beside him. "Riders coming, Jeff."

"Where?"

"From the direction of town. Seen 'em when I went out to look at the horses. Looks like six, eight of them. Posse maybe."

Jeff got up, squinted at the sun then at the barren little knoll. If it was Stumpy Grant there was probably a warrant for Jeff's arrest in his pocket. He turned to Garra. "Saddle me a horse, 'Tonio." Garra looked quizzical, waited for more and when none came hurried off. Caleb, over by the tailgate getting breakfast kept squinting up the knoll while he wrapped food in half a flour sack.

"Here, Jeff; cold meat's better'n no meat. What'll we tell them?"

Jeff hefted the sack. "Tell them anything you want to," he said. "They'll see my tracks—if they're after me."

"We'll stall 'em."

Jeff nodded over his shoulder and started towards Garra who was hastening up with the horse.

"Thanks, 'Tonio." He swung up, shot a final glance at the knoll and whirled away. "I'll be watching. When they leave I'll come back—if I can."

But he couldn't; the posse lingered at the cow camp briefly without dismounting and while Jeff watched in the distance two riders circled, searching for his sign. When they cut it they whistled and the other men left the camp, ignoring Garra and Caleb. The posse rode slowly, purposefully. Determined men who would not be deterred.

Jeff rode towards the malpais with a strong feeling within him that keeping ahead of the posse was going to force him into the same country he'd driven Epifanio Pacheco's cattle. The unique retribution didn't amuse him as it might have under different circumstances.

As he rode he wondered exactly why he was running

98

from Stumpy Grant. Because he feared the law? No; he had no reason to fear it. He hadn't shot Burt Joyce. Instinct; the range-bred wariness of the Westerner? Partly, he thought. Partly because he wanted to stay free long enough to prove, or disprove, some ideas he had. And in the darkest corner of his mind was another reason that he shied away from. Lynching. People, especially in the hot months, had a way of lynching men they didn't like, thought better off dead than alive, and legality had no part in it.

He hung back just before he entered the heat-hazed brush and tried to recognise some of the riders. He couldn't without getting close enough for them to see him, perhaps shoot at him, but he was certain a thick, squatty rider was Stumpy Grant, and that convinced him that Garra had been right. It was a posse from town beyond doubt.

The whiplash of heat burnt through the early morning hours, scourged the range, hurled waves of fury down across the spiny undergrowth, made the air scald his lungs with a bitterness reminiscent of creosote bush, and eventually his mount grew satin-shiny with sweat, his shirt darker and his eyes narrower.

But it wasn't hard to stay well ahead of Grant's posse. They rode in a long walk, boring into the sunlight as though blind to its glitter, impervious to its fury. Moving steadily, ploddingly, along his trail. In that dogged persistence he recognised the marshal's character. Stumpy was famous for never giving up on a trail. Persistence had been substituted for imagination, and persistence caught criminals. Grant was amply endowed with it.

When the country became flinty Jeff swung south, hoping to leave no tracks behind. Thirst bothered him a little as the sun hung directly overhead. When he angled down a shadowy canyon and found water in its lowest reaches he was tempted to lie down. The air was ten degrees cooler, limp with fragrant humidity, enticing. He and his horse tanked up and pushed on. From a barren ridge he watched the posse fan out, probe for his tracks and eventually swing south never hurrying. He eased his horse down off a hump and held due south with the sun beating against the side of his face as a compass.

The chase worked its slow-stubborn way all through the afternoon. Grant's possemen made every twist, every turn Jeff's trail took. At the creek they lingered half an hour and Jeff half-hoped they would give up. Then they appeared across the barren, shimmering rim of the canyon and the pursuit went on.

What had been originally a simple matter of discouraging the men from San Luis, now became something altogether different. He would never lose them by riding, so long as one of their horses could be ridden. The only alternative was to out-wit them.

He continued southward considering means of eluding Grant when the sun began its long slant towards the mountains beyond the malpais country. In the dusty distance he saw a band of Tres Cruz horses. Watching them gave him an idea.

Riding close to the horses took a long hour. They kept drifting ahead of him, curious but wary. Just before he twisted his way past the last clump of brush he dismounted, searched for a sharp-edged rock, found one, used it to hammer loose the clinches on the horseshoe nails, got a heavier, bulkier stone to hammer the shoes loose with, then twisted them off by force and hid the shoes in the brush. A little later his unshod horse tracks were mixed with the unshod tracks of the loose Tres Cruz animals and it was getting late. Let Stumpy Grant track him now!

For several hours, or until shortly before nightfall, he drove the loose stock ahead of him, worked his way in amongst them, twisted to see the tracks he left and, satisfied, smiled slightly at the perplexity among the trackers who wouldn't be able to tell one unshod hoof-mark from another. He used the horses as a screen until the shadows lengthened sufficiently, then swung off in a northeasterly direction intending to return to the cow camp and hear what Garra and Caleb had to say.

Grant's posse was nowhere in sight when dusk descended but Jeff rode warily. His lips were dry, his eyes cinder-dry. There was alkali dust on his whisker stubble and little lines of weariness fanned out from his eyes. The horse was tucked up but comparatively strong. At least he didn't hang in the bridle. He was still alert, searching the distance with interest, and when he hesitated in his stride, ears up, sniffing, Jeff roused himself quickly, a tremor of apprehension tightening his stomach.

Riding leisurely off to his right was a solitary horseman. It wouldn't be one of Grant's men—he didn't think—so it must be a Pacheco. Maybe old Juan the Indian. Prudently Jeff swung northward a little, but it was all open country. The only thing that would keep him obscured from the rider was failing light.

But it might be Garra or Caleb with news.

He reined up, made an unwanted cigarette, lit it behind cupped hands and watched through habitually squinted eyes the way the stranger went. It wouldn't be one of his men—they would have trailed the posse—or would they? Exhaling a short burst of smoke irritably he swung southward, riding slowly, letting the stranger get well ahead of him. Whoever it was, Jeff had to know. It might even be the scout of another posse.

The dusk helped hide him but it also hampered him, shadowed everything but the silhouette, and until he was within shouting distance he couldn't even make out the colour of the stranger's horse. By then they were both approaching the first bold scatterings of brush, and somewhere in the middle distance ahead would be the San Luis posse.

The stranger topped out over a gentle rise, disappeared down the far side and the night closed in with a heavy vacuum of silence. Jeff stopped, pinched out the cigarette, listened, heard nothing, and frowned. If his quarry had stopped beyond the ridge—why? The uneasiness came up again. He dismounted slowly and led his horse southward so as to come out around the slope. His heart was beating with a leaden cadence in his ears.

The night was down in full hush. At a spindly manzanita he left the horse and went on afoot. It dawned on him that if the stranger was on the ridge he couldn't turn back. A shot in the night—it wouldn't be hard to sky-line him now. Sweat started out from the exertion. He made a purposefully wide detour of the slope's lower outfall and approached the off-side from the rear. When he was as close as he dared to get, he stopped, listening, peering, and a voice spoke sharp and clear in the stillness.

"Don't move. Stand right where you are."

He only stiffened for a second then futility, anger, and disgust, all flashed over him. "You," he said flatly. "All right; I see the rifle; you can put it down now."

"Come closer—put your hands above your head."

He walked dutifully forward and when he could make out the small oval of her face, the full roundness of her figure behind the carbine, he stopped with a twisted smile.

"I ought to be horsewhipped; this's the second time. You must have eyes in the back of your head."

She made no move to lower the carbine. "What are you doing out here this time?"

Dryly he said: "There seems to be a prevalent opinion that I'm wanted by the San Luis law. Stumpy Grant's tagging along out here somewhere with six men—after me."

102

Her mouth formed a big "oh" but she didn't voice it. The gun muzzle drooped a little.

"Can I take my arms down now, ma'm?"

"Yes. Where are they?"

"My arms?"

She lowered the gun swiftly. "Don't be humorous."

"Grant's riders?" He made a sweep westward with one arm. "Out there somewhere. I was quite a ways ahead of them when I got to wondering who you were. 'Didn't want to ride smack-dab into another posse—or an ambusher—so I trailed you out."

Chapter Six

He wasn't certain because of the dullness of the night but he thought she was half-smiling up at him. When she spoke there was humour in her tone.

"Where I was raised we have lots of Indians. They teach us things now and then which occasionally prove useful—like sensing when you're being followed."

He regarded her stoically and for a long time didn't speak. When he did, his voice was almost gloomy. "If that's all they taught you to sense, you've missed something."

"What do you mean?"

"It's pretty simple," he said. "I'm in love with you." He drew in a great breath and let it rasp out into the abrupt silence. "Surprised, Lola? I don't reckon you are—maybe you're disgusted though." The hardness of his smooth face glowed like stone. "Ashamed you'd draw a man like me, aren't you? Well——"

"Don't. Don't talk like that." She was motionless, very erect, her eyes watchful, her expression strained. After a moment, as though emerging from some inner argument, she said, "Why aren't you different? Why aren't you like other men?"

His voice still had echoes of scorn in it. "What other men? The ones you've known—cowboys, clerks in stores, banker's sons? Because I never had a chance to be, I suppose."

"But you don't have to be so hard—so ruthless."

He shook his head at her slowly. "Not ruthless—not

any more, Lola. Not even hard, any more. Listen; because I *have* been something doesn't mean I always have to be—does it?"

"I don't know. I wish I did, though."

Impulsively he said, "Lola; smile at me. You were almost smiling when you got the drop on me a few moments ago. Smile now."

She saw something wistful in his face. A peculiar lonesomeness, and she smiled. Her lips faintly parted and much of the stiffness gently fell away. Still smiling she said: "Tell me on your honour—did you shoot Burt Joyce or didn't you?"

"On my honour I didn't."

"Oh; that's a relief."

"You thought I did?"

"I—wasn't sure one way or the other. That's why I rode out in the night. To be alone—to think of that—and other things."

A flickering warmth appeared in his eyes. He caught her arm, pulled a little, bent his face low, felt for her mouth and kissed her and an explosion erupted inside his head in total silence. For a second they stood close.

"Don't run from the law."

He heard without heeding. The liquid darkness of her eyes held him like stone.

"It makes you look guilty. Please . . ."

He straightened a little. "I don't like the idea of being lynched," he said. "I hear folks around San Luis are in that frame of mind."

"They hate you so much Jeff," she said softly, sadly. "That's a terrible price to pay for success, don't you think?"

"Don't preach to me, Lola. If they'd kill me standing here like this I'd be grateful to them. Y'know; I've worked hard getting what I have. Darned if it isn't all sort of valueless right this minute. Ever hear of anything crazier than a man who'd trade half his life for a woman's kiss? You're looking at one right now. One kiss . . ."

"But they wouldn't lynch you, that's foolish to believe."

His teeth flashed at her. "Is it? Foolish or not———"

"But Burt knows you didn't do it; he must."

"Burt? Has he said so?"

"He hasn't said anything; how can he, unconscious? But he will. He'll remember—he'll know."

Jeff considered it and shook his head. "He was walking away from me; his back was to me, Lola."

"Then how could you shoot him in the *side* of the head?"

He frowned a little. "Yeah; I guess that makes sense." He tightened his hold on her arm. "Go back, Lola, stay with Burt until he comes around. Be my eyes and ears in this; will you?"

"Yes."

He stood awkwardly. "I've already said I'd trade all my cattle for one kiss so I have nothing left to give for another one."

She stood very straight with her face tilted up. For a second her mouth brushed across his then she stepped back. "I can give what you can't buy," and she moved deeper into the darkness after her horse.

He watched her ride past. Neither spoke nor waved but their faces, pale, ghostly, exchanged a long look until she was gone and the sound of her horse was swallowed up in the gloom.

Very heavily Jeff went back to his own horse, fingered the cincha, swung up, reined northeast and struck out with no thoughts of the posse groping, listening, creaking its way through the dark coolness.

When he rode boldly into camp a premonition brushed across his mind. He ignored it, swung down and stood beside his horse gazing at Garra and Caleb, who were sitting up, fully clothed, on their bedrolls, watching him. Heavily he said, "Good evening, gentlemen."

Caleb's head remained towards him in a rigid, unnatural way. Antonio Garra's face worked, his mouth formed elaborate, silent words. Too late Jeff saw the 'breed's fingers patting an empty hip-holster.

"Good evenin', Jeff."

He turned very slowly towards the wagon. Stumpy Grant was behind a cocked carbine, small, thick body slightly bent, eyes like black ice in the shadows under his hatbrim.

Jeff slumped. "Hello, Stumpy. Rode around me, huh?"

The sheriff straightened out of his crouch a little; the hand crooked into a talon around the trigger lost its tenseness. "Yeah; rode around you after you pulled your horse's shoes and lost us with the Tres Cruz loose-stock. Figured you were heading back here. What took you so long?"

"Oh—I stopped long enough to change my life, Stumpy."

"What?"

"Nothing. I'm under arrest—is that it?"

"That's it, Jeff. Let go your gunbelt will you?"

"Sure."

Jeff dropped the shell-belt and gun, stepped sideways away from them. "Hope you got enough deputies to keep my neck from getting stretched, Stumpy."

"You did potshoot him, didn't you?"

"Nossir, I did not, and when he comes around he'll tell you I didn't."

"Then who did?"

Wearily Jeff said: "You're the law, I'm not. You get paid to find these fellers—find him."

"I think maybe I got him right now."

Marshal Grant kept Jeff standing and unarmed, Caleb

and Garra sitting on their bedrolls until the rest of the posse shuffled in, tired and angry-eyed looking when they saw Jeff. The men dismounted stolidly and looked inquiringly at Stumpy Grant. He flicked his carbine barrel a little.

"Couple you boys take him in tow. Put a rope around his neck and make it fast to your saddle horn. If he tries to make a run for it we'll save the law some trouble. All right; let's go. It's late and I'm dog-tired."

The group of men rode ploddingly down the night towards San Luis and in spite of his predicament Jeff couldn't find it in his heart to be more than distantly aware of personal danger. He was fully occupied with something else; something to do with the beginning of life, living, not the end of it.

When they got to town it was dark and hushed. Overhead some thick clouds rolled across the moon plunging the men, the village, the land, into alternate darkness and liquid paleness. The strong echo of their horses' hooves roused some dogs. Their barks were thin and challenging.

At the marshal's office Stumpy Grant got down and jerked his thumb at Jeff. They went into the still-hot little office. Grant cursed and cuffed a coal-lamp to life and when a deputy entered growled at him to dismiss the posse and put up the horses, then he turned towards Jeff, stared at him a moment then said, "Sit down." Jeff sat; he wondered if his own countenance looked as grey and forbidding as Grant's face looked.

Stumpy dropped into a chair, blew out a breath and slumped. Without preliminaries he began: "Listen t'me, Jeff; you been raisin' hell and proppin' it up around here for ten years or such a matter. Folks're damned nigh fed up with you and your kind. Shootin' deputy marshals is the limit."

"I told you I didn't shoot him."

Grant's small eyes grew warm. "Now tell me you never burnt out a clodhopper or you never run cattle or never picked a fight here in town." Grant's anger increased as he spoke. "You got a reputation that stinks to high heaven— you know it and I know it. I haven't heard any lynch-talk but it wouldn't surprise me any, and that's a fact."

Jeff bent his head over a cigarette, finished it, lit it and held out the sack. "Smoke?"

Grant shook his head without speaking jutted his under-lip and said, "Doc says it'll probably be weeks before Burt can talk. You didn't guess that, did you, when you said Burt'd be able to prove you didn't shoot him."

Unperturbed Jeff said, "I'll be around. I'll wait him out. All I was worried about was that he might die."

Grant stood up. "You'll be around all right. Come on— I got a real tight cage for you."

It was turning dawn when Stumpy Grant locked Jeff in. A thin edged streamer of pink light lay against the horizon. The air was blessedly cool and San Luis slumbered on except for some men down by the freight corrals who were happily swearing at drowsy mules.

Jeff considered the lumpy bunk built against the wall, sank down upon it fully clothed and closed his eyes. Sleep came instantly and he was undisturbed until men's voices outside the small, narrow window high in the back wall of his cell, vibrated in his mind, awakening him.

". . . In his cussed cow camp, I heard."

"Hah! I thought he'd be harder to catch'n that."

"Gettin' him away from Stumpy'd be risky. I got no cherish for buckshot, Sam."

"'Know what I think? I think if folks'll jest let the law work him over it'll be enough."

A loud snort of derision. "Hell; he'll get clear. Mordant's a moneyed man."

"That's what I mean," the softer voice said. "There's

on'y one thing on earth he loves—money, success. Well now, the kind of a lawyer he'll have to hire to beat this drygulching charge'll price him right out of business. Lawyers got ways of leachin' the blood right out of a rich man."

"Hmmm."

Jeff's mouth twitched. He lay on the bunk staring at the ceiling of his cell. If enough men felt the way the soft-spoken man spoke, danger from lynching was small. He sat up, made a cigarette, smoked it, letting his mind drift back over events. One among them kept crowding out the others. A mellowness grew within him—and a hunger greater than his obsession to succeed had ever been. He stood up, dropped the cigarette, stamped it out, dragged a bench close and climbed upon it to look out the window. Almost the first thing he saw was Matt Reynolds going into his office. Moments later a big hulk of a man followed Reynolds. Donnellen. Jeff's mind closed down over the significance. He dropped back to the floor and was standing, lost in thought, when Stumpy Grant came in with a white crockery bowl and coffee cup.

"Y'breakfast."

Jeff started forward to help the burdened marshal. Grant snarled at him. "Get back by the wall. Way back. Now stay there."

Jeff watched Grant put the bowl and cup on the floor by the steel-strap door, straighten up warily. "Stumpy," he said, "I've got a little story I'd like to tell you. Sit down and visit a minute." He was half smiling, the hardness gone from his eyes. Grant stood by the door watching him.

"What's it about?"

"About Burt's shooting, for one thing," Jeff said.

Grant's interest showed. He bobbed his head. "Start talking, I'm listening."

"After Burt got shot my two riders came into camp.

Antonio Garra rode up on that knoll where the old oak is and found a .30—.30 casing."

"I know that," Grant said. "I got the thing off him last night." Grant's right hand dove into a pocket and emerged with the shiny casing. "This is it."

Jeff felt around in his shirt pocket for the casing he'd salvaged after shooting Donnellen's carbine. He tossed it carelessly to the lawman. "How do their firing pins match up, Stumpy?"

Grant was silent a long time as he paired up the casings. He turned Jeff's over and over in his fingers, finally raised his head and fixed Jeff with a triumphant stare. "Twins. Both came from the same gun, I'd say. Good; now where's the fun, Jeff?"

Jeff's mouth was quirked. "You know where my carbine is, go see if the casings match up."

Grant continued to stare. "Don't be smart, Jeff. If you know something—the sooner you spill it the sooner you get out of here."

"I'm comfortable, Stumpy."

The marshal's face reddened. He went out of the cage, slammed the lock and shot Jeff a waspish look. "All right stay here until you rot," he said, and stumped back down the corridor to his office.

Jeff didn't move. He was smiling a little. Carefully he took out his watch, punched the stem and when the face opened he gazed at the hands still half-smiling, and put the watch away.

It took an hour of waiting but Stumpy came back, stood outside the cage glowering. "Ready t'talk?" He asked.

Jeff laughed outright. "Quit acting, Stumpy. You're not running a bluff on me. Don't act so domineering. You're more worried about me not talking than I am and you know it."

The marshal's face flamed but he controlled his words. "Listen t'me, Jeff——"

"You listen. If I don't tell you who owns that other gun——"

"How do I know you even *know* who owns it?"

"I do. I fired it to get that casing. I know who owns it all right—so I know who shot Burt, don't I?"

Grant leaned on the cell. His voice changed quite abruptly. "What's the sense of all this mystery, Jeff? You and Burt always sort of got along."

"Sort of," Jeff repeated dryly.

"Well then—unless you put this feller up to potshooting him, what's the secret?"

"No secret, Stumpy, I just want to do a little stick-whittling."

"Like what?"

"Let me out of here and do what I tell you for ten hours and I'll not only prove to you I didn't shoot Burt but I'll show you the man who did shoot him."

Grant straightened up again. He was silent for a moment. "Jeff; dammit all; you know I can't turn you loose. Why, the whole town knows you're in here. They'd have my topknot so quick——"

"I understand, Stumpy," Jeff said in mock sympathy. "You'd better not waste any more time. Folks'll be after your topknot quick enough if you don't get your evidence against me right soon."

Marshal Grant stood like stone peering through the steel slats at Jeff. He swore in a thick, exasperated tone. "By golly, Jeff, you listen to me . . ."

Jeff turned his back, stepped up on the bench and rested his arms against the rammed-earth wall peering out the little window as though Stumpy Grant were miles away in the heat-simmering distance.

Grant's anger dwindled, got choked down, and after a

withering silence he said, "Jeff; get rope-wise. You *know* I dassen's turn you loose, boy."

No reply.

"You're obstructing justice, Jeff. That's a real serious charge. You can go to prison for that."

Jeff's attention was abruptly caught and held by two men talking under the overhang near Waters's store. The shorter, harassed looking figure was Al Waters. The taller, more massive figure belonged to the Federal Land Inspector, Cliff Donnellen. Behind Jeff, Stumpy Grant's voice droned on.

". . . Get caught sure as the devil. You're a marked man —anyone who saw you'd know you wasn't supposed to be loose. Be sensible, Jeff."

Jeff got down off the bench. The pleasant feeling of moments ago was gone. He'd overlooked something. Donnellen's purpose in San Luis; his condemnation proceedings against the Pacheco grant. Donnellen had obviously been waiting for Matt, earlier. Now he was deep in conversation with Al Waters. There would be only one outcome from those meetings and that was ruin for the Pachecos and closer, more immediately vital to Jeff, the loss to him of Lola Valdez.

". . . Went with you, Jeff. Maybe tonight—after dark. How's that sound?"

Jeff looked up at the lawman. "What did you say? I was thinking of something else."

"I said I'd let you out on the condition that I went with you."

"When?"

"Tonight, after it gets dark. We'd both get caught sure as the blue blazes in broad daylight." Grant's voice turned hopeful at the quick look of interest in Jeff's face. "If we're seen I'll just up and say I'm takin' you back over the scene of the crime. I'm going to warn you right now though—

if you try to get away you'll come back tied across your saddle and that's a promise."

"Make it earlier," Jeff said, ignoring the threat. "At sundown."

Grant squirmed. "All right. Now Jeff, by God you'd better produce . . ."

Jeff sank down on the bunk unheeding. Stumpy stood a moment indecisively then went back down the hallway towards his office.

The knotty problem was Donnellen's condemnation approval. Jeff himself had set it up. No one knew any better how entirely legal it was. The Pachecos didn't have enough livestock to warrant the land they claimed, and until he'd told Lola of the impending suit against the grant they'd had no warning of disaster. No time to sell cattle to fight back. Further, he knew that old Epifanio would be ignorant of how to fight such a battle. When he'd originally planned the condemnation all those things had been factors in his favour. He'd recognised them as such. Now each one was a pitfall which he had to struggle over to forestall Reynolds and Waters. And—there was the matter of Donnellen. Of them all he stood out as probably the most dangerous. Next in point of danger was Matt Reynolds. Lastly, Al Waters's avarice alone kept him in the fight.

Jeff made another cigarette and smoked it hunched over, unaware of the passing of time. When the shadows slanted long and narrow through the little window he didn't see them lengthen.

Granting that he could overcome Donnellen's ambushing abilities; granting that he could swing Stumpy to his side, and granting that he could win over old Epifanio—Reynolds and Waters still had an iron-clad method of getting at least sixty thousand acres of the Pacheco grant.

He was still pondering ways to circumvent this when

Stumpy Grant came bobbing down the hallway, spurs ringing in the hollow stillness.

Jeff looked around and upward. Grant was stooping a little as he fumbled with the lock. He spoke without looking up. "Come on; let's get going. I won't rest easy until this is over with."

The door swung inward and Jeff arose, passed through and waited for Stumpy. The marshal hung the lock on the hasp and his fingers lingered reluctantly.

"I'll need a gun, Stumpy."

Grant came fully round. His face was screwed up adamantly. "In a bull's eye you will," he said aggressively. "Any gunning gets done I'll do it."

Jeff shrugged and started for the office. Grant hurried forward and hissed at him. "Not that way, you idiot. It isn't dark out yet. This way."

"You got two horses?"

Grant was picking nervously at a long unused rear door. He answered gruffly. "Did you think we was going t'ride double, mebbe?"

Outside the day was dying in a shroud of grey light and the air was cool and strong range smells lay in the humidity. Two horses were tied close in the shed behind the jail and Stumpy Grant's face was shiny with sweat when they were mounting. More to himself than to Jeff he said, "I never done an underhand thing in m'life I didn't get found out about it. You watch and see." He looked accusingly at Jeff. "All right; now what do we do?"

"First let's ride for Pacheco's."

"Pacheco's . . ."

"Yeah. It'll be dark by the time we get there. After that we'll come back here and arrest Burt's drygulcher."

Grant made a sound deep in his chest. "He's here? In town? By golly we'll take him first."

But Jeff reined around without speaking and when they

were clear of the shed he shook his head at the marshal. "We'll do this other little chore first—or we don't go."

Grant followed Jeff without speaking but his face mirrored doubt and wrath in equal parts until they were well down the alley and reining out over the range, then he relaxed a little. Jeff rode with the reins slack, making a cigarette. When he finished he held out the sack and Stumpy grabbed it, worried up a cumbersome cigarette and leaned far over to get a light from Jeff's match.

They rode in silence until full darkness lay over everything then the lawman sighed, spat, and swore a sizzling oath. "What're we going out to Pacheco's for—or shouldn't I ask such a personal question?"

Jeff's eyes crinkled. "You can ask. Tonight you're going to back my play and I expect to need your badge before it's over with. We're going to ask a lady to do us a favour."

"What lady and what kind of a favour?"

"Miss Lola Valdez—old Epifanio's niece. We're going to ask her to pay a man a visit so we can get close enough to grab him before he grabs his gun."

"Burt's potshooter?"

"Yeh."

"Hmmm. Who'd that be? Not Epifanio or his son?"

"Nope."

"Well—your man Garra, mebbe, or that stringbean outlaw you call Caleb?"

"Nope. Just relax, Stumpy."

"Relax! Me with my neck out a yard—relax!"

Jeff rode silently through the soft silence. Once, he saw a flaming star arc down the firmament making a scratch on infinity that died almost before he could blink. Later, coyotes out seeking something dead or helpless, called back and forth to one another as they hunted. When the man-smell came down to them they dropped into instant silence, testing the night air for direction, standing like

116

stone, sly, wise, eyes beady with challenge and wiliness but not fear.

Jeff reined up when he saw the spilling lamp light ahead. Held his reins carelessly and made out the dim paleness of the Pacheco house with a brooding look deep in his eyes.

"Now what?" Marshal Grant asked.

Without taking his eyes from the house he said, "You ride down there and fetch her back up here."

Grant swore. "In a pig's eye," he said swiftly. "What do you take me for, anyway."

Dryly Jeff said, "That's beside the point right now. Some day I'll tell you though. Listen, Stumpy, if I rode down there they'd have me nailed to the wall—unarmed and all, like I am. Don't worry, I'll be right here when you get back."

Grant swore some more, and squirmed. "Your word, Jeff?"

"My word on it."

Grant urged his horse ahead without looking back. Jeff watched him go, eventually stepped down, loosened his cincha, made a cigarette, lit it within cupped hands and hunkered with the slack reins trailing from his fingers.

It might be hiding behind a girl's skirts, he thought, but it was the surest way to take Donnellen. There was a time, not too long ago, that he'd have scorned such a ruse but now he wanted to live, wanted to avoid risk. Just the same his conscience pricked him when he thought of Lola being anywhere near. But he wanted Donnellen alive and Lola was the best assurance he had that the Federal man wouldn't go for his gun.

He heard a horse whinny and guessed Stumpy was stepping down at the house. What would the marshal say to get her to ride back with him? A resourceful man wouldn't find that much of an obstacle and until he heard two horses coming through the darkness it didn't occur to him that Grant might simply have told her the truth. He knew that had happened, though, when he saw her face, with anxiety not surprise, staining it.

"Jeff."

He held up a hand to swing her down. Stumpy sat there looking from one to the other with a dawning understanding spreading across his features. Under his breath he said something in a mildly surprised tone, too low for either of them to hear.

"Jeff; I don't understand—this." She motioned towards the marshal.

"It's simple enough, Lola. I've got a favour to ask you. It may be a mite unpleasant to you."

"What?"

"This feller Donnellen . . ."

"What about him?"

"Have you seen him lately?"

"No; for a few days he was at the ranch. I don't know where he is now. In fact, I haven't thought about him."

"Well," Jeff said, "he's staying at the Emerald Slipper Hotel, Lola, and I'm pretty sure he's the feller who pot-shot Burt."

"Oh—but no, Jeff. Why should he?"

Jeff threw a glance at Marshal Grant who had made a startled sound. He dropped his eyes to the girl's face again. "Because the way I've got this figured Donnellen was hired by Matt Reynolds and Al Waters to ambush me, after I backed out on the agreement to get your uncle's grant condemned."

"But why Clifford Donnellen, Jeff?"

A shrug. "He's the Federal land appraiser from Raton, Lola. Mostly, men get that job to pick up bribes. I've been told it's the best paying business in the Southwest. I'm guessing Donnellen's one of that kind. I've got other reasons, too, but we talk about them later. Will you go visit him in his room at Emerald Slipper, keep him occupied—keep his attention diverted long enough for Marshal Grant and me to get the drop on him?"

"Yes; surely." Her black eyes were unwavering. "When?"

"Right now."

Her mouth formed a silent Oh. "My uncle will wonder if I'm gone that long. I told him I wouldn't be gone very long, Jeff."

Without any hesitation Jeff said, "You can ride back and tell him you'll be out a little longer, can't you?"

"Yes, I suppose so. Jeff?"

"Yes'm?"

She half turned from him. "Nothing. It would sound silly."

He moved closer. "What? Nothing you would say would sound silly."

But she went to her horse and mounted under the quiet stare of Stumpy Grant. "Wait here, I won't be long."

They watched her ride away and Stumpy got down, adjusted his saddleblanket with meticulous care, then peered at Jeff across the saddle seat.

"I never would have believed it, Jeff."

"Believed what?"

"You and that lady . . ."

"Oh, shut up!"

Stumpy fidgeted with the blanket, tugged up the cinch and turned the horse around so that it was behind him; he was facing Jeff. "By golly I'm glad, though. Y'know—I was married once." In the face of Jeff's dour silence Stumpy Grant's benevolent enthusiasm engulfed the marshal, curled the corners of his hard mouth and softened the flake-greyness of his eyes. "It's better'n the cow business, believe me, boy."

"You've got more to worry about than me and Lola."

Briefly Stumpy's hardness reappeared. "Yeah," he agreed. "Seems that I have. So it was *that* feller's gun you copped the other casing from, huh?"

"Yeh."

"Well; why'n hell didn't you just tell me back in town and we'd of surrounded the hotel and———"

"And got a damned war going and maybe got Donnellen killed. Where would that leave me, Stumpy? With him dead I couldn't *prove* I didn't shoot Burt."

"Uh-huh," Stumpy said pleasantly. "And if you was locked up you couldn't come out here and see *her* either, could you."

"You simpleton—I'm after Donnellen right now."

Stumpy wasn't altogether convinced. He was still hugging the amazing discovery to his heart that tough, ruthless, Jefferson Mordant, terror of the San Luis range, was in love, when Lola came loping out of the night, hauled up and looked squarely at Jeff.

"I'm ready now. Uncle Pifas won't worry."

Stumpy swung up with a puzzled expression. "Uncle who?"

"Pifas; that's an abbreviation for Epifanio."

"The hell it is," Stumpy said dubiously. "Epifanio's bad enough. A man was to call me a—Pifas—why, I believe I'd fight him."

Jeff reined close to her, caught the soft flash of her teeth when she smiled at him and saw a soft blur of movement. She was holding her hand out to him, low. He reached over instinctively and felt something cold and hard. He looked down. It was a blue-black six-gun. He couldn't repress the grin as he took it wordlessly, tucked it into his waistband and gazed thoughtfully at Stumpy's back, then laughed softly. The marshal shot him a quizzical look, shrugged and faced forward again.

"Lola; you're wonderful."

"No," she said, "protective."

Jeff raised his voice. "Stumpy; ride ahead a little farther, will you?"

The marshal didn't reply but urged his horse deeper into the night and Jeff swung closer to Lola so that their stirrups rubbed.

"You've changed your mind about me?"

She looked away from him, into the gloom. "It isn't that easy. The things I've heard—I believe—are mostly true, Jeff." She turned her head, gazed directly at him. "But I don't think they are the things you'd do—normally."

He pondered a moment and when he would have spoken she interrupted his thoughts.

"I think a lot of things have contributed to your hardness but I don't think you're really hard—not so that kindness—maybe more than kindness—wouldn't bring out more of what you are underneath. Does that make sense? I'm not very good at expressing my thoughts." She looked embarrassed.

"You know what made me go against my former thoughts? You. Sure; I wanted the land—I still want it—but not as badly as I want you. If losing the land puts me even close to getting you, then the land can go . . . only, Lola, when I started this thing I did it knowing your uncle wouldn't stand a chance against a re-appraisal, so I may lose yet. I will lose, unless I can think of some way to beat my own original planning. Do you see?"

But she didn't reply. Very slowly her head swung away from him and for the balance of their ride into San Luis she said nothing. He rode beside her feeling miserable, alternately hating himself, Matt Reynolds, Al Waters, and the dishonest Federal land agent, and seeking ways of circumventing what seemed sure-fire.

At the edge of San Luis Stumpy Grant reined up and

waited for them. He was quick to see how they rode, she handsome, very solemn, almost tragic looking, Jeff grim and unhappy appearing. Stumpy toyed with his reins thinking unique thoughts for a lawman, but Lord! she was a beauty. You could put Anglo-Saxon women on horses until Doomsday but they never had the grace, the unconscious ease and suppleness of Spanish girls a-horseback. Stumpy had an unsuspected streak of romanticism in him a yard wide and he would have died protesting that he possessed no such a tomfool thing.

When they were close Lola reined up. Jeff's horse came to a halt of its own volition. He straightened in the saddle. Thoughts tumbled through his head. A peculiar desperation was on him. So much depended upon the next few hours.

"Well?" Stumpy said quietly, then he saw the gun-butt sticking slantingly out of Jeff's breeches and inhaled a sharp breath, opened his mouth and closed it, tightly. All those miles and no bullet in the back . . . Let it go.

"Stumpy," Jeff said. "Donnellen didn't shoot Burt because he thought Burt was me, for nothing. Sure—we had a little tiff, but you don't drygulch people over things like that."

"So?"

"So; I want to know for certain who put him up to it."

"Naturally. Why do you say 'for certain?' Got some ideas?"

"Yeah. If you're going to break a lariat you hunt for the weakest strands, don't you."

"Yup."

"Then you go around to Al Waters's place and arrest him. Scare the hell out of him. He'll scare easy I think. Make him think you're after him for attempted murder—Burt's—but don't tell him anything else. Understand?"

"Well," Stumpy said, "That much, yes. What's the rest of it?"

"Take him down and lock him up. Leave him there alone with his conscience until we're through, then we'll sweat it out of him."

"Sweat what out of him?"

"Who hired Donnellen to shoot me when he mistakenly shot Burt."

"Oh! Waters'd know, you reckon?"

"I'm betting it was Matt Reynolds, but to prove it I want more than Al Waters. I want Donnellen alive, so Lola and I'll wait here for you to return after locking Waters up. All right?"

Stumpy's eyes dropped to the blue-black gun and stayed there briefly. He raised his shoulders and let them drop. "All right," he said.

Chapter Seven

"Jeff?"

He stepped down from the saddle before answering and faced her across the spindrift of darkness holding up his hand for her to dismount. She swung to earth and swept up close to him. He thought the stillness of the night had a golden quality.

"Jeff?"

"Yes'm."

"What is it in a man that makes him attractive to a woman?" She asked it naïvely, looking intently up at him, the fullness of her figure a soft, rich shadow. He shook his head.

"I don't know. I can't even say exactly what it was that made me see you as I do—that first time."

"But—the things I know about you . . ."

"Know or heard?" he asked ironically.

A tiny shrug. "If there is some falsehood, there are also some things I've never heard about too, aren't there?"

"I suppose so," he said solemnly. "What do those things matter? There is truth between us, Lola."

"I can't get rid of my doubts, Jeff."

"And you can't make things change by just wanting them to change," he said in a curiously soft way. "I know."

She saw the moonwash carve his features from the night. "There is bitterness in you."

His eyes smiled gently. "Not bitterness, Lola. I don't resent some of the things life's done to me. But I've worked out a way to strike back, and it's made me pretty well off. Hardness, maybe, but not bitterness."

"You know yourself better than I ever will, I think."

His eyes grew very still. "Will you try to know me, Lola?"

She was motionless and the night around them seemed to draw back a little, hold itself suspended while she turned fully and slowly towards him, face tilted, with a dark splendour in her eyes. "Yes; if you ask me to."

"Will you marry me, Lola?"

"I will marry you, Jeff."

He kissed her, felt the tremor pass over her, felt the singing softness of her mouth, the supple goodness of her body close to his. Then she pushed a little, stepped back.

"Jeff—all those other things—if they don't work out right—my family . . ."

"I understand," he said. "They'll be angry at you. Your uncle——"

"You never knew—I argued for hours with my uncle to get him to sell you some of the grant. I used every means I could think of to persuade him. His answer was always—no. He would die before he'd give up an acre of the ground his people have always owned."

"And Ramon?"

"Ramon?" she said on a rising note. "He's more like us; like you and me."

"Then it's too bad he doesn't own the grant."

She looked briefly troubled. "But Ramon dislikes you, too."

In a strong way he said, "The whole damned world can dislike me if it wishes—so long as you don't."

"Jeff . . ."

He felt her hands on his arms, fingers tightening, hurting a little through the fabric of his shirt. Moving slowly he put his arms around her. "All these troubles—you'll see—they'll fade away like a mirage, Lola. They've got to, because I've already gotten the reward. For that reason I know——"

"Listen!"

He heard the horse coming at a slow walk, turned his head and waited to catch movement. She stirred in his arms but he didn't release her. With a swift lowering of his head he kissed her squarely on the mouth and released her as Stumpy Grant rode up, drew rein, gazed owlishly at them and yawned.

"I got him."

"Any trouble?"

Grant shook his head. He looked tired and slack-bodied. "Naw. Like you expected he was scairt pea-green. I hinted all around about Burt's drygulching an' he swore like seven devils claiming he didn't know anything about it at all."

"I think," Jeff said, turning towards his horse, "that he's a liar. Well; let's go."

Lola mounted swiftly and pulled close to Jeff looking over at him. He swayed in his saddle, lay one hand over her fingers on the saddlehorn and drew his hand away after one intimate quick squeeze.

"Honey; when we get to the hotel you'll go up the front stairs first. I'll be behind you a little ways."

"What shall I say to him?"

"Tell him your uncle wants to see him right away— now, tonight. He'll ask what for and you tell him your uncle was counting out a lot of money when you left, but that you don't know exactly why he wants to see Donnellen. I'm guessing he'll think your uncle knows that Matt's paying him to condemn the grant, and is going to up the ante to prevent it."

"Well, but——"

"Say," Stumpy interrupted. "Just where've you got me cached while all this is going on?"

"You're going across to the livery barn, Stumpy, and

turn his horse loose and cache his saddle. Then you'll get in his horse's stall and when he comes up———"

"I'll get the drop on him."

Jeff nodded. "How does it sound?"

"Like a damn," the marshal said, pleased.

"But, Jeff," Lola said. "He'll put on his gun when he leaves the room. Wouldn't it be better to arrest him in bed—unarmed?"

Jeff smiled without humour. "Fellers like Donnellen aren't ever unarmed, Lola. They sleep like a coiled rattler. We don't want shooting. Aside from the chance that Donnellen might get killed, one of us might—or some roomer in the hotel. Those walls aren't much thicker'n a cigarette paper; I know."

Lola subsided but the anxiety on her face lingered. Seeing it, Jeff said: "You'll tell him you'll wait downstairs by your horse until he's dressed. Don't forget that. I don't want you anywhere around when we close in on him. Understand?"

"Yes. Where shall I go?"

Stumpy said: "Go down to my office, the door's never locked. Go in there and stay away from the windows."

She looked inquiringly at Jeff. He nodded and altered his reins a little so that his horse turned south on the dark roadway and went down through San Luis in the dead silence as far as the livery barn's side-corrals. There he stopped, sat perfectly motionless gazing up at the Emerald Slipper Hotel. Stumpy hauled up behind him and Lola's horse stopped voluntarily.

"All right, Lola. Our horses will be out of sight so he shouldn't suspect anything, but if he does—if you don't like the looks of things—when you come downstairs again, light this match then throw it away." He handed her a match, changed his mind and handed her several more.

Without speaking the girl nudged her horse on down

the roadway. Jeff dismounted, stood beside his horse watching her and when Stumpy tugged Jeff's reins out of his fingers he let them go reluctantly, showing in that way how little he liked having Lola mixed up in what might easily become a brief but savage gun battle.

For some obscure reason Stumpy spoke in a coarse whisper. "I'll put the horses out back. They'll be tied to the wash-rack behind the barn. All right?"

"Yeh. Stumpy; damn you don't misfire on this, now. Get his gear hidden and turn his horse out somewhere—anywhere, just as long as it won't be in the stall when he comes for it."

"Don't worry," Stumpy said testily. "Y'act like this is the first surround I ever pulled. Hell's bells; I was doing this when you were——"

"All right; go do it then. She's going into the hotel."

"I thought you were going in with her?"

"Not with her—after her. Get moving."

Jeff crossed to the east boardwalk and went softly down it, hesitated at the stairway, listened, heard nothing and entered the narrow passageway and began mounting the steps. He was half way up, surrounded by an impenetrable darkness when he heard voices above, stopped still and listened. The words weren't distinguishable but the voices were and he recognised Lola's. Donnellen sounded garrulously surprised, even a little suspicious, Jeff thought. He dug his nails into the banister and waited. If Donnellen refused for *any* reason at all . . . Then he heard Lola's small spurs tinkling and let his breath out in relief, turned and went gingerly down the stairs and out on to the plankwalk. When she emerged from the stair well he spoke her name and she started, turned towards him with a gasp. Her face looked unnaturally white in the gloom.

"You frightened me."

"I'm sorry. Is he coming?"

She moved over beside him. "Yes; but I said I'd wait for him at the livery barn instead of here." She saw his face cloud up. "Jeff; if I wasn't by my horse when he came out —don't you see?"

"I reckon. All right; now beat it down to Stumpy's office."

She moved, then stopped, cast him a sidelong look. "Just like that?"

He smiled, bent low and kissed her, touched her hair with the fingers of his left hand, then gave her a gentle shove. "Go on, honey." She went.

Jeff re-crossed the road down a ways from the front of the hotel. His spurs sounded faint in the muffling dust. Long glances at the town showed only more darkness. Even the dogs were silent. A little fingerling of summer-night-breeze scurried around his ankles and patted at the dust before hurrying on. The livery barn's doorless entrance was huge, square, and stygian. Jeff found a deep shadow down from it and melted into the slit between two buildings where it was darkest.

A strong tension seemed to come out of the night and envelope him. He cast a squinted glance down towards the marshal's office, knowing when he did it he couldn't see, wouldn't have been able to had it been broad daylight because the office and livery barn were on the same side of the road. Waiting, he had tantalising thoughts about Stumpy, cast them out as being ridiculous and kept watch on the hotel entrance.

When his patience was the thinnest after what seemed an inordinately long wait, a bulky shadow surged on to the plankwalk, paused, then crossed the boards with sturdy steps, went down into the dust of the roadway and began an angling course towards the barn. Lola's horse, still tied to the hitchrail before the hotel, turned its head leisurely to watch the progress of the man.

Jeff drew the big, new Colt from his waistband. Its grip was cool against his palm. With one digit hooked over the hammer he waited. There was a temptation to step out and stop Donnellen now; maybe force him to draw, and wing him. He fought it down and only his eyes tracked the big man as he, unsuspectingly, entered the barn.

Jeff moved swiftly and silently. When he was at the edge of the entrance he stopped, listened, heard muttered oaths in the saddle room and waited until Donnellen came out. The big man stood wide-legged, his head low, eyes perplexed and angry, then he started towards the stall and Jeff slid into the barn and pressed deeper into the darkness as he moved along the wall.

He was close enough to see the squat, burly figure raise up when Donnellen's right hand lay upon the door latch. Out of somewhere a wet glimmer of light shone off Stumpy's gun and Jeff plainly heard Donnellen's breath cut sharply into the stillness. Jeff spoke a fraction of a second ahead of Stumpy.

"Put 'em both up over your head, Donnellen. Make one funny move and you're coyote bait."

The words weren't loud. They scarcely carried to the end of the barn where the night man was sleeping blissfully unaware that he wasn't alone in the old building, and Donnellen obeyed but it took him several grudging seconds to get his arms up. Stumpy kicked the door back and moved out and around the much larger man. With fingers that flicked like a snake's tongue, he plucked away Donnellen's gun. Jeff moved in closer. Donnellen turned his head a little, squinted hard, then swore.

"Mordant!"

"Who'd you think?" Stumpy said dryly. "General Harney, mebbe?"

"Turn around."

Donnellen turned, fixed them both with hating eyes and

130

finally let his gaze rest on the lawman. "Workin' with criminals, eh. Well; when my report about *this* gets to Raton, you'll have a bucket full of hell on your hands, Marshal. You can't molest Federal men and get away with it—let alone run with fellers like———"

"Aw, shut up," Stumpy said disgustedly. "You're a hell of a one to talk. Usin' a Federal job as a cover for drygulching. Why———"

"Wait a minute, Stumpy," Jeff said. "What did you mean, Donnellen—'when my report about *this* gets to Raton?'"

"Just what I said. You're an outlaw and he's a———"

"Have you sent some other report to Raton?"

Donnellen blinked, moved his arms a little and Stumpy's gun tilted back.

"Well?"

"Sure I did. That's what I'm up here for."

"About the Pacheco grant?"

"Yes; what about it?"

"What did you say in it?"

"That's none of your damned business. Government affairs———"

"I'll find out," Jeff said, ramming the gun into his waistband and starting forward. "I'll kick it out of you, Donnellen, like I kicked some bullying out of you once before."

Stumpy Grant danced sideways. A slow, sly grin broke over his features. "'Don't know what this is all about but like I've always said—never interfere when a big man gets picked on."

"Hold it, Mordant. Hold on. I'll tell you what it said—not 'cause I'm scairt of you, but so's you can eat your lousy heart out. I confirmed that the Pacheco grant is three times as large as the Pacheco family needs for the stock they run—or ever have run. How do you like that?"

"I don't," Jeff said, stopping, hands dangling at his sides. "Now tell me how the law works on those things. How do the Pachecos beat that finding?"

"How?" Donnellen laughed gratingly. "They don't. There'll be a hearing and when it's over about sixty thousand acres of the grant will be ordered up for sale."

Jeff glared in rigid silence. Finally he said, "How much did Reynolds and Waters pay you for that, Donnellen?"

"I don't know what you're talking about. Marshal—if you got a charge you'd better take me in, because I'm going to have one of my own to prefer."

"'That so?" Grant said amiably. "Like what?"

"Obstruction of a Federal officer for one. Incompetence in office, for another. Need any more?"

Stumpy's smile lingered. "Yeah; find me one that's as good as attempted murder."

"What're you talking about—you old fool?"

"About the way you bushwacked Burt Joyce, my deputy marshal."

"You're crazy," Donnellen said roughly.

"Mebbe, but I got enough to make it stick."

"Like what?" Donnellen demanded in the same tone of voice.

Jeff interrupted. "Like Al Waters for one thing. You should've known he's afraid of his own shadow where guns and trouble are concerned."

Donnellen's gaze swung slowly to bear on Jeff, He looked and probed then faced the marshal once more. "Take me in or turn me loose. I've listened to about all this bull I aim to."

Stumpy shot Jeff an inquiring look. The cowman stepped aside and jerked his head. Donnellen began to move. Over his shoulder he said: "With my arms up like this?"

"Yeh; with your arms up like that. Go on."

They went down the plankwalk towards Grant's office

and when he was entering Jeff heard a rooster crow some-where in one of the back streets. He waited just outside the door until Stumpy had turned up the lamp, then turned and looked towards the east. The sky was as black as ever. He shrugged and went into the office in time to catch the venomous glare Donnellen shot at Lola. The girl avoided the big man's face and moved around him beside Jeff. She groped for his fingers, found them and let her hand lie within his hand.

Stumpy looked grey-weary but pleased. In an almost genial voice he asked the land man if he'd like to tell them about the drygulching, and reaped a scorching denial of complicity. Stumpy stood there and just stared—then he shrugged and sank down on to the chair behind his desk, indifferent appearing.

"Suit yourself." He fished out the two casings. "Look. See these? One of 'em's the casing from the shot that downed my deputy. The other'n's one Jeff fired out of your carbine. They're identical. Blow *that* through your beard, Mister Big."

"Doesn't prove anything," Donnellen said. "Say; how long do I have to stand like this? My arms're gettin' tired."

"So's my tail-end," Stumpy said "from sittin' here listening to you lie. You can put 'em down when you decide to tell us exactly how and why you potted my deputy."

"That's unlawful brutality, Marshal. I'll——"

"You'll quit bluffing—that's what you'll do—or your cussed arm'll wither up and drop off for all I care. Now; why did you shoot Burt Joyce?"

"I didn't shoot him,"

"How much did someone pay you to do it?"

"No one paid me to do anything up here."

Stumpy looked at Jeff, who moved around so that he was facing Donnellen. Lola remained behind the big man. Jeff's beardstubble made his smooth, bronzed face look much older and leaner.

"You want to know what Al Waters told us, Donnellen?" Jeff asked.

Donnellen snorted. "Who're you tryin' to buffalo, Mordant? When did *you* talk to Waters—or anyone else, for that matter, except this lawman who runs with renegades?"

Jeff turned, went to the cell-block door, opened it and peered down the corridor. Twisting his head he beckoned. "Come here, Donnellen. That's good. Now look down there where that lamp's hanging. See him? Now get back." Jeff closed the door. He had a feeling of triumph. It showed in the saturnine half-grin on his face. "He was right easy to talk to, Donnellen. One of the easiest men I ever kicked a confession out of."

Donnellen's eyes drifted away from Jeff's face. They went to the wall, up it, along the ceiling as far as Grant's desk then down to the marshal's face. "You'd better lock me up, Marshal," he said in a sullen-stubborn way, "because you can let this bucko beat on me all day and I won't tell any of you a cussed thing!"

Jeff moved aside shrugging and Stumpy got out of his chair gruntingly, went towards the cell-block door beckoning Donnellen. Jeff watched them and said, "Stumpy; bring Waters back with you." The marshal nodded without speaking.

Lola looked anxious. She crossed to the edge of Grant's desk and leaned on it looking at Jeff. "What can you do with him now?" she asked.

Jeff felt for his cigarette makings, bent his head in thought as his fingers worked. Slowly he said, "There's more'n one way to skin a cat, Lola. If he won't talk Waters will—I think."

"And if Waters won't?"

He lit the cigarette and beheld her over the match. There was a shade of exasperation to his glance. "We've always got Burt to fall back on—to wait out—if we have to."

Her anxiety heightened. "Jeff," she said softly. "Donnellen said he'd already sent his report on the grant."

He looked puzzled. "Well?"

"Don't you see? Unless you're cleared of the Joyce shooting you'll be in jail. We won't have anyone to help us fight to keep the grant."

A slow sensation of futility seeped into him. "That's right," he said. He was still lost in thought when Al Waters came through the cell-block door. Jeff eyed him wickedly. Stumpy slammed the door with unnecessary force and sighed, headed for his chair and dropped down into it with a careless wave of his hand. "He's all yours," he said to Jeff.

Jeff kept the merchant pinned down with his stare for a full minute. Very slowly he turned towards Lola and said, "Honey; why don't you wait outside? This might not be very pleasant to watch."

The effect was achieved when Waters back-pedalled to a bench along the wall, sank down upon it and protested in a strained voice.

"Jeff; I didn't have a hand in anyone gettin' shot. You know me better'n that." He threw up a defensive hand, gestured with it.

"But you'd steal their land."

Quick as a flash Waters said: "That was your idea, not mine."

Stung, Jeff's face reddened. He inhaled deeply off his cigarette. "You know Donnellen, don't you?"

"Know him? Not exactly. The first time I met him was this morning on the walk outside my store. He just said Matt wanted to see me."

"What did Matt want?"

"Money," Waters said unpleasantly.

Stumpy Grant was listening with a frown. He leaned forward on the desk and touched Lola's arm. "Say; just what's this all about, anyway; this other stuff they're talking about. The grant, and so forth?" Lola bent low and in a whisper began to tell Stumpy the whole story.

Jeff could hear them in the background, and ignored it. "Al," he said, "how much money have you given Matt so far?"

"Few thousand—but it wasn't to hire——"

"No, of course it wasn't. Donnellen just tried to kill me and hit Burt Joyce in error, for target practice." The brooding eyes were inflexible. "Anyone who incites drygulching is as guilty as the man who does the shooting—in my eyes."

Waters's upper lip showed moisture in the lamp light. He swallowed hard and held the silence, looking glassily at Jeff.

"Now tell me Matt didn't want me shot."

The silence still held. Jeff's upper lip raised a little. "Go ahead, Al—tell me that."

"I don't know *what* Matt wanted, Jeff, but you know I'm averse to violence, And drygulching—why—I wouldn't get mixed up in anything like that. I've got a position; a business . . ."

It sounded convincing. Jeff's mind was tired, his body sagged in spite of him. Suddenly he turned away from Waters, met Stumpy Grant's gaze and shrugged. "I could get more out of him but you wouldn't like my methods."

Grant shook his head. "No," he said firmly, "I wouldn't." He looked at Waters. "Do you admit being part of this land-squeeze deal with Reynolds?"

"It's perfectly legal," Waters said quickly.

Grant nodded his head a little and said, "Sure it is. So's

136

shooting armed robbers in the back—but *men* don't do either one. All right; one more question: Do you know anything at all about Burt Joyce's shooting?"

"No," Waters said in a stronger voice.

"Then," Grant said acidly, "get off your duff and let's get you locked back in the cooler."

When the marshal was gone Jeff stubbed out his cigarette and swore under his breath. Lola watched him, something like despair in her expression. When the marshal came glumly back into the room he fired a short glance at Jeff. "Now what," he said. "It'll be daylight in another couple hours, Jeff. You got to be under lock and key by then, y'know."

"But we're on the right track, Stumpy. You can see that can't you?"

"Yes, I can see it, but we'll have to move slow from now on. You'll have to think things up and I'll have to be the dog-robber—the errand boy for you."

"Time," Lola said softly. "Jeff? How much do we have? If he sent the report off even as late as today it'll be in Raton tomorrow. When will the government people down there hold the condemnation sale?"

"I don't know, honey. I've never seen this done before."

"Haven't you," Stumpy said. "Well; I have. They'll hold that cussed sale by the end of this week. You can bet your bottom dollar on that."

Jeff went to the door, cracked it a little and gazed into the east. There was a thin edging of paleness. The air smelt of dawn; it was sharp and fragrant. He closed the door and said, "Stumpy; there's one thing left."

"It'd better be real good, boy," the marshal said.

"Reynolds."

Stumpy was unimpressed. "Hell—excuse me, ma'm—heck, Jeff; if you couldn't sweat it out of Donnellen or wishy-washy Al Waters how'd you expect to get it out of Matt?"

"I'm going to try," Jeff said, and when Stumpy stood up with a resigned expression Jeff shook his head at him. "I'll do this one alone."

But Grant wagged his head. "You can't. Besides, it's goin' t'be light out pretty quick now . . . I'll go along. We got t'hurry though." He looked at Lola then back to Jeff. "'Want her to wait here?"

Jeff nodded without looking at Lola and when Stumpy had his hat on again and was moving towards the door Jeff smiled wistfully and held up his crossed fingers. "Say a prayer for us, honey."

Outside on the plankwalk Stumpy said, "From the way things are going, Jeff, you're going to need more'n a prayer. You're going to need the Lord's direct intervention—as they say in law courts."

A feeling of frustration was churning deep in Jeff. He walked along beside the marshal, head down, feeling the initiative draining out of him. Two raffish dogs were scenting up the side of the road; they paused long enough to consider the two men then resumed their way. Stumpy looked towards the east. When he spoke it was to voice in the rangeman's way something he lacked the vocabulary to describe adequately.

"Look at that sky, Jeff. Dawn's the prettiest time of the day."

Jeff threw an annoyed glance at Stumpy and ignored the dawn. When they came to the break in the main roadway of San Luis which led off down one of the haphazard side-streets, Jeff turned towards Reynolds's house. He slowed, waited for Stumpy to catch up, and stopped. "This time you cover the back," he said. "I'll go in the front."

It sounded normal enough. Stumpy nodded indifferently, never suspecting that Jeff might have another reason for wanting him to be outside the house while Jeff was inside. He slapped at a mosquito on his forehead and screwed up his eyes. "That's the house yonder, Jeff."

"I know. I was there to see Matt not long ago."

Stumpy looked up suddenly. "Say; Miss Valdez said originally this land-grant business was your idea. You ought to be ashamed of yourself, Jeff."

"I am, Stumpy."

Taken aback by the suddenness of Jeff's contrition Stumpy said no more until they were one house east of the Reynolds's place. Then he thrust his head forward and lowered his voice. "I'd best cut off here, Jeff, and make for the gate in the backyard fence." He straightened up as a new thought struck him. "Say—does Matt have a dog, d'you know?"

"I've never heard one," Jeff replied, then smiled. "I hope, if he does have one, it's as big as a pony with teeth like razors."

Stumpy looked around and upward in a startled, injured way. "Well now," he said. "Aren't you a hell of a friend."

Jeff's teeth flashed. With one hand he urged Stumpy on his way. "Go on. I'll wait here until I see you're through the gate."

Stumpy made his way warily beside the house as far as the fence. He put a hand on the tall gate and strained to see over it before entering. The gate was solid planking and too tall. Stumpy lowered his head, lifted the latch and ducked through. Jeff listened but there were no sounds. He swung his attention back to the house. It was dark and uninhabited looking. No light, no sound, no movement. Fine, he thought, that's as it should be at four-thirty in the morning.

He went through the little picket-gate in front, up the stone walk and on to the porch. Through a partly open window he caught the scent of stale cigar smoke. He rolled his knuckles over the door. A rooster crowed in a wavering, cracked voice. Others took up the endeavour and, incongruously enough, a tom-cat let off a series of complaining yowls. He rapped again, harder, and stepped up close to the door listening. The third time he knocked the windows rattled and that time a man's voice called out blisteringly.

"What's the hell's so important it won't wait 'till daylight?"

"A fire," Jeff called back, raising his voice several octaves.

From within the house came the vibration of feet being slammed into boots. Steps, wide and solid, echoed. The door was flung open and Matt Reynolds in breeches, boots, and with his night-shirt tucked carelessly, hastily, into his breeches, stood there glaring puffily at Jeff. "Oh," he said, "It's you. What's afire, Jeff?"

"Nothing that I know of," Jeff said affably. He moved forward, used the palm of his hand to push the skeletal form of Reynolds back into the house. "I didn't say there was a fire, Matt. I said a fire was important enough to wake a man up about, before dawn."

Reynolds's face was murky with suspicion and doubt. "You didn't come all the way in from the cow—Say, by God; aren't you supposed to be in jail?"

"Yeah; that or drygulched, Matt."

"Don't start that drygulching business again, Jeff. We went all over that the last time you were here."

Jeff reached out and pushed. It wasn't a blow yet it had weight enough behind it to send Reynolds backwards into a chair. He glared at Jeff. "What the hell's got into you? I——"

"I'll do the talking for a minute or two, Matt, you just listen. First off, I'm free because the marshal's got a couple of prisoners who pretty well exonerated me for Burt Joyce's shooting." He watched Matt's face. The sunken eyes blinked but that was all. "Want to know who they are? Al Waters and your potshooting Federal man, Donnellen."

"Not *my* man. Jeff——"

"I said I'd do the talking. You hired Donnellen to potshoot me at the cow camp. He didn't know me well enough at a distance and mistook Burt Joyce for me. How much did that mistake cost you, Matt?"

"I don't know what the hell you're talking about."

"Yes, you do. Just like you know you bought Donnellen to go along on the Pacheco grant. We both know that, Matt."

"That wasn't my doings. You steered me into that."

"And I told you to drop it too, remember?"

"People don't drop free money, me or you or anyone else."

"Not even Donnellen," Jeff said. "How much did Burt's shooting cost you?"

Matt's face got fiery red. The tight skin shone. His hands moved in their jerky way as he sought to rise. Jeff leaned forward and put one large hand against him. "Don't get hostile, Matt. I'll stomp it out of you."

Matt subsided but his eyes were venomous. Normally afraid of men like Jeff Mordant, he was ruled now by the greed that had motivated him from the start in the Pacheco land grab. Very slowly he leaned back in the chair. One hand lay inert in his lap, the other hand was wedged between his trouser pocket and the chair. His nostrils quivered slightly.

"Jeff; I told you whatever went wrong at your end I'd get straightened out for you. I'll still do that. But by God you nor anybody else is going to make me let go of the Pacheco deal."

"You're wrong, Matt. Dead wrong. The deal is blown sky high. I blew it up myself."

Reynolds made a sharp grunt of derision. "You couldn't. In the first place Donnellen's findings have already been sent in. In the second place I dictated them myself and he endorsed them. Signed them so that there are no loopholes. The grant will be condemned, ordered up for sale in less than five days."

Each word hit Jeff in the raw. Reynolds couldn't help but see that he had scored for Jeff's face looked slack, his eyes despairing.

"And another couple of things, Jeff, since you're going to buck me four ways from the middle. I've hired a damned sharp lawyer down Raton way to make sure our bid's accepted." Reynolds leaned forward, the hand at his side straining against his leg. "It's all legal so far as the government's concerned. Every cussed bit of it. I'll give you another ringer too. Al and I've got that sixty thousand acres sold for spot cash." He sat there, hanging forward in the chair, a bitter light of triumph showing from his eyes. "And when that fool of a town marshal let you out of jail he gave his job away. I'll have the town fathers fire him before noon today. Now get out!"

Jeff went closer to the chair. "The marshal's safe enough, Matt," he said gently. "You ought to wish you were half as safe. Get up, Matt. Come on, get up. You're going to tell me all about Burt's shooting. After that we'll talk about the grant. Right now that's more important to me."

"More important? Why; are you a deputy now, too?"

"Because when you're through telling me how much you paid Donnellen to drygulch me, I'll be in the clear."

Reynolds rose. He was wearing an acid smile. "I thought you said Stumpy had Donnellen and Waters in jail now?"

"I did. He's got 'em both locked up."

"Oh. But they haven't told him anything. That's it, isn't it?"

"Maybe. They haven't told him enough, let's say."

The bony grin widened, became more solidly satisfied appearing. "So you're here to get the facts from me. Well —go ahead and try it, Jeff."

There was too much confidence in Matt's tone. Jeff started to take a step closer before he saw the reason why. Reynolds's hand was moving away from his trouser pocket. The long, thin fingers were wrapped around a murderous little .41 under-and-over derringer.

Matt watched Jeff stop in mid-stride. The dangerous smile deepened. "Come on, Jeff. You've got a reputation for tackling odds. Try this at ten feet!"

Chapter Eight

Matt couldn't miss. Firing blind at that distance it would have been impossible for him not to hit Jeff. The room was full of dark violence and silence. Jeff raised his eyes sardonically to Matt's face. One corner of his mouth was quirked. "What's that prove, Matt? It might save you from a drubbing, temporarily, but that's all. You're in trouble to your ears."

But Matt was scornful. "I'm not in trouble. You and that half-wit town marshal are. You'll both wish to God you'd left well enough alone before you're out of this. I promise you that, Jeff."

"Put that toy down, Matt."

The bony face glistened. "Sure; after you get out." The long fingers tightened around the big-bored little gun. Confidence showed out of Reynolds's eyes like fire.

Jeff gazed steadily at the thin man. He was surprised; more than that, he was coming to a conviction that he had underestimated Reynolds's temper. "I said put it down."

Matt's face held its hardness. In a grating way he said: "Don't make a mistake, Jeff; I'm not fooling. You forced your way in here and I've got the right to put you out. I'll shoot if I have to."

Jeff had no doubts. He felt like swearing. There was no fear in him of the little gun or of the man, but there was disgust that he had allowed himself to be caught unprepared. He could raise his voice and call Stumpy, but if he did that the marshal would keep him from getting anything out of Reynolds in the only way Reynolds could be made to talk. He took a deep breath and expelled it, gazing steadily at Matt.

"You're forcing me, Matt."

"The only thing I'm doing," Reynolds said in an even voice, "is protecting myself from an intruder—a criminal who's supposed to be in jail. It'll be justifiable killing if you force my hand; you know that, Jeff."

Sideways, Jeff thought. . . . Sideways and try to cold-cock him before he can swing his wrist. Poor odds; a big body at ten feet moving sideways, against Matt's wrist which would only have to move six inches to track him with the little gun. The under-and-over had two bullets. Damned poor odds.

Quite suddenly a dazzling shaft of new sunlight splashed into the room, made Jeff acutely aware of the dwindling hours of freedom. He had overstayed his time. Lola had said, "If you're locked up you can't help us. . . ."

He moved fluidly in a sideways plunge. A deafening explosion rocked the room and Reynolds's voice cried out incoherently. Jeff was slammed off balance by a breathtaking impact in the side. He lost his balance and went over backwards, fighting for balance and spinning. When the second gunshot came ringingly he was falling. The bullet went over him, made a tearing sound as it struck the far wall.

Jeff clawed at the Colt in his waistband, got it out and swung it. An impact that made pain sear up his arm tore the gun from his grip and sent it careering, skittering across the room. He saw the big boot's follow-through, understood what had happened and rolled crab-like to escape the fury of the boot. Reynolds was wide-legged after the kick.

Somewhere out back a man's voice yelled something indistinguishable to the combatants, then a thunderous drumming shuddered through the house as Stumpy hammered on a locked door.

Jeff's breath came short. There was an unnerving numbness in him. When he saw Matt bending to retrieve the Colt he rolled frantically to intercept him. The thin man groped, missed, turned with a fierce curse and aimed another kick. Jeff threw up his arm, fended off the blow, gritted his teeth at the pain and grabbed desperately at the leg. Cloth slid through his fingers. He locked them around it and held on. Matt lunged to get free. Jeff held on and threw his prone weight sideways and Matt crashed to the floor. Jeff released his hold long enough to fling himself half upright and down upon the wildly threshing figure. He felt Matt's bony torso squirming under him and a blindly thrown punch bounced off his temple.

Matt Reynolds was no match for Jeff, normally, but now Jeff had difficulty making his body obey his mind. He felt sluggish, lethargic and fought his enemy like a drugged man. The big arms were clumsy, the rock-hard fists inaccurate. Twice he missed Matt's face and crunched his knuckles against the floor.

Matt derived hope from Jeff's awkwardness and fought like a savage. Blood dripped from Jeff's nose and ran in a trickle from the corner of his mouth. He absorbed the rain of blows, but fortunately the numbness prevented him from feeling their pain.

The seconds fled by while the strange fight continued and quite gradually Jeff's numbness wore off. With its passing came the sharp, sticky agony from the bullet wound. With it also Jeff's co-ordination returned. He sucked back from a looping blow and went low under another, cocked his fist and thudded it into Matt's chest. The thin man ceased his wild struggles for a second, then gaspingly redoubled his efforts to extricate himself. With a monumental spasm of effort he managed to throw Jeff off and struggle part way to his feet. Jeff rolled once, pressed stiffly against the floor and came up first.

When Matt straightened up he walked into a murder-

146

ously slashing punch that knocked him completely off his feet. A rickety old chair broke under him, its shattering sound doubly vivid in the room's silence, broken only by the whistling breath of the combatants.

Jeff felt the numbness returning, running up his right side to the shoulder and down it to his foot. Wisely, he stood erect, spraddle-legged above the Colt pistol, waiting. But Matt wasn't coming up. He lay twisted and broken looking amid the chair's wreckage. A great purple welt was puffing to life along the slant of his jaw.

"Get up, Matt, I'm just warming up."

Matt neither replied nor moved. Jeff dragged his numb leg after him. Went over and bent a little. Matt's eyelids quivered, his breath was low and laboured. Jeff bent, grasped the nightshirt's yoke and heaved Matt upright. The unconscious man didn't weigh much but he hung limply. With a grunt Jeff let him fall, went painfully back, retrieved the Colt, rammed it back into his waistband and limped through the room to the kitchen. At the dipper and water bucket he paused long enough to hear Stumpy's blows raining indiscriminately upon the stout back door. With a crooked smile he dipped up water and ignored the external sounds, went back to the parlour and flung the water upon Reynolds. His aim was poor. Most of the water drenched Matt's clothing, very little found his face. Jeff made two more trips before Matt groaned, flickered his eyelids and tried to sit up.

Jeff tossed the dipper aside. Its landing made Reynolds jerk in surprise. When his sunken eyes focused on the dipper they didn't stop there but went to the thick legs beyond, up them to Jeff's grey looking face with its whisker-stubble and lethal, deadly-blank expression.

"I said get up, Matt."

Reynolds sat a moment longer then turned on his side, used both hands and pushed himself upright. He staggered to a chair and slumped into it working his jaw, running fingers over the swelling and shaking his head gingerly.

"You ought to know better than to try and kill a man with one of those toy pistols," Jeff said. "Now stand up. Since you're so damned full of fight I'm going to give you a bellyful. *Stand up!*"

But Matt Reynolds stayed down. He shook his head some more, squinted around the room confusedly and looked at Jeff again. "No more," he said.

Jeff made a sharp little laugh. "No? You think you can shoot me, try to get me drygulched, try to ruin me in other ways, and just say 'no more' and I'll forget it all? Guess again, Matt. I've just started fighting you; just started."

He took two painful steps, dragging his right leg, towards the chair. Reynolds watched him approach soberly, ran his eyes down the lame leg and back up to Jeff's face. "I got you, by God."

"Yeh; you got me." The big fists curled, knuckles stood out white and bony. "We're about even now so stand up and let's see what you can do against a crippled-up feller."

Matt's eyes became dazedly speculative, assumed a fuzzily sly look and he put both hands on the arms of the chair and pushed himself upright. Jeff moved swiftly, summoning his failing strength to get close. His right arm curved up and outward. His body was twisted, crouched behind the blow and Matt didn't see the fist until it was too late to duck from it. He took the blow flush in the chest and, because he was leaning forward didn't go over backwards but slid down to the floor the second time, in a bedraggled heap. His mouth was open. Air went raspingly in and out in broken little sobs. Strangely, he didn't lose consciousness.

148

"Come on," Jeff said. "Try again."

But Matt Reynolds was whipped. He coughed and spat and leaned back against the chair he'd risen from with his head hanging, wagging from side to side negatively.

"How much did you pay Donnellen———"

"Hey—dammit! What's going on in here?"

Stumpy came boiling through the kitchen door with his pistol up and balanced, the hammer back. He stopped just inside the parlour and looked from one of them to the other, mouth agape.

"Jeff; you're shot!"

Jeff ignored him. "How much did you pay Donnellen to drygulch me, Matt?"

Reynolds's head lifted groggily, swung around so that his lacklustre eyes hung appealingly on Stumpy Grant.

Jeff went closer and reached down, caught Reynolds by the front of his nightshirt and lifted him bodily to his feet. "How much—damn you—before I———"

"I don't remember," Reynolds said hazily. "Paid him couple thousand I think. Paid him . . ."

Jeff pushed him into the chair and looked over at Grant without speaking. The marshal eased off the hammer of his gun, holstered it and crossed the room heavily to stand before Reynolds. "Say that again," he ordered. "You hired Donnellen to potshoot Burt?"

"Yes, I hired him, but not to get Burt," he looked up at Jeff "To get *him*. I thought he'd recognise him. He told me they'd had a fight."

"That was in the dark," Jeff said. He looked at Stumpy. "That's what I figured happened. Donnellen was up on that ridge. Burt and I're about the same build. Donnellen saw Burt walk towards his horse at my cow-camp, thought it was me and blasted him."

Stumpy was looking down at Reynolds. "Is that it, Matt?"

"That's it," Reynolds said.

Stumpy turned away from him. "Jeff; is he armed?"

"No. See that little toy in the corner there? That's what he had. It's empty now."

"Then let's look at your wound."

Jeff twisted a little, held his torn shirt to one side and sought the injury. When he saw the scarlet stain on his thigh he grunted. "Thought it was lower. Down in my leg somewhere."

Stumpy squinted at the torn flesh and made a silent whistle. "A little higher and inward and you'd have had a hole in you big enough to toss a cat through. Look at the powder-burns on your breeches, man. How far was he when he fired?"

Jeff shrugged. "What's the difference? You got enough to arrest him for attempted murder and turn me loose?"

"Sure," Stumpy said. "Set down there and watch him until I go get a buggy for you."

Jeff sat and Stumpy left muttering to himself. The minutes dragged by. Matt gradually recovered himself. They looked at one another for a long time in silence. Finally Matt said: "All right, Jeff; you made it. You got off the hook and got me on it. But paying a man to dry-gulch someone won't get me hung—especially since the man who got shot didn't die. But there's one thing you'll never pull off—the Pacheco deal will still go through like I planned for it to."

Jeff felt unutterably tired. "We'll see about that," was all he said.

Reynolds felt his swollen jaw, opened and closed his mouth several times. "You won't be going to that sale, either. Not with a hole in you."

"I can hire a lawyer down at Raton to do that for me."

"All right," Matt said. "How'll you get around my prior rights as the man whose ordered the sale?"

Jeff looked sardonically at Reynolds. "*Your* prior rights —why hell—*I'm* the one who first ordered up that reappraisal and you know it."

Matt tried a cold smile that failed. "You dropped out. I had that written into Donnellen's report and he signed it like that. I'm the only adjoining land owner with prior rights now." The sunken eyes shone with hating triumph. "The law says the first adjoining land owner who calls out the sale gets first—and last—bid, on condemned landgrant property. Donnellen told me that himself. That's when I had him say that you'd dropped out and that I then had prior rights."

Jeff's growing weakness made him easy prey for despair. He studied Reynolds's face for a hint that he might be bluffing and found none. The dregs of defeat soured him. "Matt," he said in a very quiet way, "I've never killed a man yet that I didn't think was better off dead. You're going to die like that if you force this land grab through. I mean it, Matt, every damned word of it."

Stumpy Grant arrived back at the house with two impressed deputy marshals. He found Jeff and Matt locked in a cold and penetrating silence, each looking as grim and bruised as death itself. He motioned towards Matt with a casual glance. "Put irons on him, boys, and one of you stay with him in the buggy. Now then," he said to Jeff, "we'll carry you out and———"

"I can walk." Jeff got up. The angry pain began running up and down his right leg. "Just take me to the doctor's place, Stumpy."

"Well—all right. Want me to send for your two riders to haul you back to the cow camp?"

Jeff looked surprised. "Cow camp? Hell, man, I'm going down to Raton in the morning."

It was Stumpy's turn to look startled. "Raton? Man; you'll be doing good if you can climb the steps to your room at the hotel. You'll be abed for a few days and after that you'll be on a cane for weeks. Raton hell!''

He limped to the livery buggy, leaned heavily on it to get in and kept his jaws locked all the way to the doctor's office. There he lay like a stone staring at the ceiling while the medical man cleansed and bandaged the wound, got up, paid the doctor over his protests, and walked back outside.

San Luis was alive with excitement. People passed him with frankly curious stares. A few bolder ones approached him. He ignored them and let the sun beat down upon his back and shoulders. It felt good, invigorating. He went to an overhang post, gripped it with one hand and eased down off the boardwalk into the inches-deep dust of the roadway. Angled across towards the marshal's office and was navigating the step up on to the far walk when he saw Lola come out of the office and start hurriedly up towards him. He held on to the overhang upright and waited for her, unconscious of how dirty, bedraggled and haggard he looked.

"Jeff!"

She took his free arm and lifted it, held it tightly while her black eyes sought his grey ones. "The marshal told me. I was on my way to the doctor's." Her grip tightened. "Oh —you shouldn't be out. I'll help you to the hotel. Marshal Grant said you had a room there. We'll——"

"Lola," he said quietly. "Did you see Reynolds?"

"Yes. He laughed at me. Told me he'd won regardless of what you'd done. Marshal Grant told him he had another guess coming, that *he'd* lost, not you."

"Well," Jeff said slowly. "Stumpy was talking about Burt Joyce's shooting. That's only incidental to what you and I're worried about. Matt meant he'd won on the land grab."

She searched his face. "But he hasn't, Jeff—has he?"

Jeff leaned against the upright. Behind her he saw people standing around in little groups, talking. The town was bathed in a cool brilliance; it was too early for the lemon-yellow sunlight to work its wrath upon the land yet.

"Has he?"

Some horsemen came loping down the roadway. Jeff opened his mouth to speak when one of them called out something vibrant and harsh, in Spanish. Jeff turned his head to look. It was Epifanio Pacheco, Ramon, and the Indian Juan; with them came Antonio Garra and Caleb. The leathery visaged old Spaniard was erect in his saddle, hawk-eyed looking, dangerous. A carbine lay athwart his saddle-swells, a big pistol hung loosely from his narrow waist. Jeff said, "There's your uncle, Lola."

She saw the riders at the same time the five horsemen saw Jeff and reined sharply over towards him. They flung to a dusty halt and swung down. Garra and Caleb, scowling, hurried forward, took places on either side of Jeff and stood stiffly mute.

Old Pacheco stepped up on to the plankwalk. Ramon beside him. He looked quickly at Lola and some of the fire died out of his gaze to be replaced with a terrible coldness. "Are you all right?" he asked the girl. She nodded, still holding Jeff's arm.

"I'm terribly sorry, but if I'd told you I was going with Jeff you wouldn't have liked it."

"Liked it?" The old man said distantly, his black eyes swinging to Jeff. "I would have forbidden it."

"But I had to. It had to be proven that Jeff didn't shoot Burt Joyce."

"And has that been proven, then?"

"Yes. Mister Donnellen shot Joyce thinking he was Jeff. A Mister Reynolds hired Donnellen to do it. Jeff——"

"Is this true, Mordant?"

"It's true," Jeff said, "and I'm sorry I had to use Lola to make it work out. I didn't mean to keep her out all night."

The old Spaniard's coldness remained unchanged. "And

now that you have used her," he said. Jeff felt anger running hot inside him at the words. "Now that you've used her—I suppose you are finished with her."

Jeff returned Pacheco's stony, hostile look. "I'm going to marry her, Pacheco," he said. "Maybe I owe you some kind of an apology for that, too, or maybe an explanation, but whatever it is I'm still going to marry her."

The black eyes moved very slowly to Lola's face. "What have you to say to that, Lola?"

"It's true, Uncle." She said no more and for a moment there was silence. Then Epifanio laid a hand gently upon the butt of his pistol and gazed at Jeff.

"You have taken my land, now you take my niece. Even if her father has no objection—I do have. I know you, Mordant; I know you too well to stand for this. Aren't you satisfied that you've ruined me but you must carry your hatred this far too? I have never killed a white man—now I will. You leave me no choice. I will not see her life ruined by marriage to a man like you."

Lola moved closer to Jeff. "Stop it," she said. "Ramon; stop him. None of you know anything about this. Jeff almost got killed trying to stop Reynolds from taking your land, Uncle. He told the marshal he was going down to Raton today to be at that sale."

The black eyes were saturnine. "Naturally. So he could buy the land."

She shook her head vehemently. "No; don't you understand? He's risked his life to stop this condemnation. Don't any of you understand?" She said piercingly, looking from her uncle to her cousin. Ramon looked more bewildered than angry. He moved closer to his father's gun arm. Garra's beetling, dark face was impassive. His muddy eyes never blinked, never left the Spaniard's face. Caleb was sharp-eyed stiffly alert appearing. Only Jeff seemed relaxed. Weariness lay in him as solidly as rock.

"Listen, Pacheco," he said. "I started this mess. All right; I'll admit that. Your niece changed that. I've been trying to stop it since I talked to her. *I will stop it.* I don't exactly know how but I've got money—if that's what it takes, then I'll use all that I have to do it." Jeff ceased speaking all of a sudden. His eyes narrowed in thought. He turned to Lola. "Honey; Stumpy's been through these condemnation proceedings—knows all about them—go get him, will you; I've got an idea."

Lola acted undecided. She looked at the men around her, saw the way Ramon was standing beside his father, closely, knew that he did so in order to back his father up or to stop a rash act. When their glances crossed Ramon nodded his head up and down at her gently. She let go of Jeff's arm and passed among them on her way to the marshal's office.

No one spoke until Stumpy came back. He looked harrassed and irritable. With rude shoulderings he pushed in beside Jeff. "Now what the hell's going on *here*," he said pointedly, irascibly. "I got troubles four ways from the middle—what you fellers tryin' t'do—stir up some more?" He glowered around then peered through sleep-hungry eyes at Jeff. "What is it, Jeff?"

"You said you'd been through these land condemnations before, Stumpy."

"That's right. A dozen times at least. Remember, I was around right after the U.S. took over this southwestern country. I'm no spring chicken."

"You said today they'd hold that sale right away. Matt Reynolds said the same thing."

"Sure they will. What about it?"

Jeff put all his weight on his sound leg and stood hip-shot. "Well; is there any way for Epifanio to keep his land? What I'm getting at is there a loophole somewhere that you'd know about?"

Stumpy gazed at Lola thoughtfully for a moment, then down at his boots. He creased his forehead, puckered up his mouth in a silent whistle and finally looked with shrewd calculation at Jeff. "I think there is," he said. "It'll depend on you. I've seen this done once before. Thirty or forty years ago. It worked."

"What is it?"

Stumpy had the attention of all of them but his glance never left Jeff's face. "If the Pachecos had enough cattle to use all their land, they'd be able to justify ownership. 'You understand what I'm gettin' at, Jeff?"

The silence came down over the little group in layers. As understanding came to each person their eyes left Stumpy and went to Jeff. He said, "Yes, I know what you mean." Epifanio made a sound and put up one hand. Jeff ignored the gesture and turned towards Lola.

"Will you run one more errand for me, Lola?"

"Of course, Jeff."

"Go in the livery barn there and borrow a pencil and a piece of paper."

She was twisting around when Stumpy dug a splinter of pencil from his shirt pocket and a sweat-stained slip of paper from the sweatband of his hat. He held them up mutely. Jeff took them, turned to use the upright and laboriously wrote out a bill-of-sale for every head of cattle his last tally showed he owned. When he finished with it he read it over, handed it to Lola to read and when she looked up slowly, incredulously, he took it from her and handed it to Epifanio Pacheco. The old Spaniard held it in his hand without once glancing down at it. His black eyes were riveted to Jeff's face. In a soft, bewildered tone he said, "This can't be, Jeff. A man doesn't do things like this."

"This man does, Epifanio. You own over two thousand head of cattle not counting your own stuff."

"But—I couldn't begin to——"

156

Jeff bobbed his head at the bill-of-sale. "See what it says? Value received in full. That means they're already paid for, Epifanio. Paid in full."

Ramon found his voice after a struggle. "What do you mean?" He asked.

Jeff nodded his head sideways towards Lola. "Her. Your approval of our marriage."

Old Epifanio was thunderstruck. He looked at Lola. She smiled at him and inclined her head gently. Pacheco looked down at the bill-of-sale for the first time and as though the words stung him looked quickly up again. "I can't do that, Jeff. Lola alone can say who she'll marry. You know that."

"Yes, I know, and she's already agreed to marry me, so I guess all you have to do is smile at us both for the cattle. That's cheap enough isn't it?"

The hand holding the paper shook. Pacheco began to close his fingers around the scrap of paper with a slow and relentless movement. Jeff reached over and stopped him.

"Don't. You need that bill-of-sale to save the grant."

"Ah. But I can't take your cattle."

Lola said: "Then just use them, Uncle. Use them with the bill-of-sale to save the grant. Afterwards give them back to Jeff."

Ramon grasped the idea long before his father did. He smiled widely and deliberately, almost diffidently, held out his hand towards Jeff. "I'm sorry about a lot of things, Jeff. My father is too."

Jeff took the hand, pumped it once and let it drop. Shyly he said, "You'd make a good cousin-in-law, Ramon."

Then Epifanio looked at Stumpy and the marshal snorted at him. "Cuss it all, man, he's giving you the only excuse that's valid to save your place. In your boots *I'd* say thanks!"

Epifanio made the embarrassed, bewildered little sound

again. "Ahhh. Mordant—Jeff—I don't know what to say."

"Nothing to say, Epifanio. I reckon we've been neighbours long enough. Being sort of shirt-tail relations might be the best thing that ever happened for both of us. Of course, you could do me a favour in this . . ."

"Name it!"

"Well; sort of go down to Raton and talk to Lola's father. Sort of smooth the trail for me down there."

"I'll leave tomorrow. No—I'll leave tonight—this afternoon." Dark blood returned in a rush to the old man's dark face. "And I'll record this bill-of-sale while I'm down there."

"Good," Stumpy said. "That'll spike the condemnation sale. There won't be any. Reynolds and Waters and Donnellen are licked to a fare-thee-well."

Epifanio wagged the limp paper. "As soon as this is over I'll give this back to you. No; I'll do better than that; I'll give you back another bill-of-sale right now, but you must keep it a secret until after the sale is called off."

Lola took Jeff's hand and held it tightly. "Uncle; we'll follow you to Raton within two days. Jeff and I can be married at our house down there."

"*Pobrecita*," the old Spaniard said in Spanish. "Then you love him this much?"

Also in Spanish she said: "Formidably, Uncle. More than life."

Lauran Paine who, under his own name and various pseudonyms has written over 900 books, was born in Duluth, Minnesota. His family moved to California when he was at an early age and his apprenticeship as a Western writer came about through the years he spent in the livestock trade, rodeos, and even motion pictures—where he served as an extra because of his expert horsemanship in several films starring movie cowboy Johnny Mack Brown. In the late 1930s, Paine trapped wild horses in northern Arizona and, for a time, worked as a professional farrier. Paine came to know the old West through the eyes of many who had been born in the previous century and he learned that Western life had been very different from the way it was portrayed on the screen. "I knew men who had killed other men," he later recalled. "But they were the exceptions. Prior to and during the Depression, people were just too busy eking out an existence to indulge in Saturday-night brawls." He served in the U.S. Navy in the Second World War and began writing for Western pulp magazines following his discharge. It is interesting to note that all of his earliest novels (written under his own name and the pseudonym Mark Carrel) were published in the British market and he soon had as strong a following in that country as in the United States. Paine's Western fiction is characterized by strong plots, authenticity, an apparently effortless ability to construct situation and character, and a preference for building his stories upon a solid foundation of historical fact. *Adobe Empire* (1956), one of his best novels, is a fictionalized account of the last twenty years in the life of trader William Bent and, in an off-trail way, has a melancholy, bittersweet texture that is not easily forgotten. In later novels like *The White Bird* (1997) and *Cache Cañon* (1998), he showed that the special magic and power of his stories and characters had only matured along with his basic themes of changing times, changing attitudes, learning from experience, respecting Nature, and the yearning for a simpler, more moderate way of life. The film *Open Range* (Buena Vista, 2003), based on Paine's 1990 novel, starring Robert Duvall, Kevin Costner, and Annette Bening became an international success.